WEIRD GOLF

18 tales
of fantastic, horrific,
scientifically impossible, and
morally reprehensible golf

by
Dave Donelson

WEIRD GOLF
18 tales
of fantastic, horrific, scientifically impossible,
and morally reprehensible golf

ISBN-13: 978-1475122244
ISBN-10: 1475122241

As Time Goes By appeared in *Blind Curve*, 2011

Aside from historical and public figures,
all characters in this work are purely fiction
and are not intended to resemble anyone
living, dead, or otherwise.

Custom editions of *Weird Golf* are available for golf outings or other groups

For information, contact Donelson SDA, Inc.
44 Park Lane, West Harrison, NY 10604
www.davedonelson.com

Table of Contents

A Word From The Author

I'm a golf writer by trade, so I spend way more time than is healthy hanging out with people who play the game, both professionals and amateurs. I've found that even the most "normal" golfer is a little odd. Has a couple of wires crossed in the old Brainiac, if you know what I mean. Why else would someone scream at a little white ball for four hours and call it fun? What other explanation is there for calling what comes out of bagpipes music? If every golfer isn't at least slightly whacked, how do you explain the mass delusion that we can all play like tour pros if we just throw grass into the wind before every shot and check the line of every putt from all four sides? I tell you, we're all candidates for the loony bin.

"Golf is played mainly on a five-and-a-half-inch course—the space between your ears," according to Bobby Jones. His audience of hackers, duffers, chili-dippers, sandbaggers, and golf miscreants undoubtedly chuckled knowingly when he said it just like they do today whenever it's repeated.

But what if that five-and-a-half-inch course in your head is twisted a little bit? What if it was built on top of an ancient Indian burial ground? Or has a nineteenth hole that only the most morally degenerate foot wedgers are allowed to play? Or what if that space between your ears is regularly visited by little blue gnomes, Superman, werewolves, or cart girls who just can't stand your smarmy comments anymore? Then what?

Then you, my friend, play weird golf. Stuff happens to you on the golf course. You notice things other golfers miss. Like when you reach into the cup to retrieve your ball, a pair of beady eyes stares back up at you. And when the moon is full, you not only seem to hit your drives a long, long way, but you have to shave twice before your wife will let you be seen in public. When you stand over the ball, heart full of hope and brain full of vaguely-remembered swing tips, you're the guy (or gal) who sees something pale and slimy crawling across the fairway right where you're aiming. And no, it isn't Carl Spackler stalking a gopher.

If you see stuff like that—or think you see it—or, even worse, want to see it—you will recognize yourself in these stories of Weird Golf.

* * *

I've made many friends playing the game of golf. I hope they still like me after reading Weird Golf, especially those who might accidentally recognize themselves among the characters in the stories.

In addition to apologizing, I'd like to thank several people, too. Not for helping with the book—everything in it is entirely my fault—but for enabling me to play and enjoy golf as much as I do. First comes my wife, Nora, who puts up with all kinds of nonsense from me in addition to my golf addiction. Thanks also to Ralph Martinelli, publisher, and Esther Davidowitz, editor in chief, of Westchester and Hudson Valley Magazines, who entrust me with the annual Golf Guide and make it possible for me to play more golf than any man should be allowed. Additional thanks to the Metropolitan Golf Association, the Metropolitan Section of the PGA, and to the Metropolitan Golf Writers Association for affording us all many opportunities to play and celebrate the game.

* * *

This book is dedicated to Dick Crumpton, whose last round ended much too soon.

~ Dave Donelson

Yuri Shoots Par

Yuri Glnstrxmlpghyq desperately needed to play golf. He didn't particularly want to, but he was absolutely required to learn the game.

"If you are going to blend in to the indigenous population, you must play their games," said the Great One shortly after Yuri was sent to the planet Earth. "Your cover as a middle-aged suburban male dictates that you play golf. You have one week to learn to play the game correctly. If you can't score what they call 'par' by next Saturday, I am going to revoke your privileges." He paused, then added ominously, "all of them."

In the Advance Reconnaissance Corps of the Imperial Intergalactic Legion, in which Yuri was a corporal on his first interplanetary assignment, having your privileges revoked didn't mean you couldn't watch TV for a week. When the Great One revoked your privileges, your body's atomic structure was forcefully de-coalesced until it disintegrated into a cloud of amorphous matter that dispersed among the miasma of the universe. It wasn't pleasant.

Yuri didn't want that to happen, but he wasn't particularly worried. After all, he was a fine product of advanced breeding technology and the representative of a superior civilization. Already, in his first two days on Earth, he had slipped unnoticed into his cover like a hand into a slipper, to use a metaphor phrased in the vernacular he picked up so easily. He bought a snazzy car on credit using the manufacturer's rebate as a down payment, moved into an over-sized house on an under-sized lot with a no-tell mortgage secured online, and found a good dead-end job in a mind-numbing cubical just like the ones his neighbors went to every day. On the second day, Yuri considered acquiring a wife, but he couldn't see the purpose. Besides, he had learned in his research that wives often generated psychological obstacles to golf and the other middle-aged suburban male activities he was supposed to emulate. Instead of a wife, Yuri bought a wide-screen plasma TV. He had acquired everything of importance.

The only thing required to complete his cover was learning to play golf, and Yuri was sure he could do that fairly easily. After all, if his pot-bellied, cigar-puffing, arteriosclerotic neighbors could play the game, why couldn't a fine specimen such as Yuri? The Great One arranged his test, making a tee time in Yuri's name at Centurion Hills Golf Course for Saturday morning. All Yuri had to do was show up and play a round of golf in which he scored par, which the Great One said was defined simply as "the standard number of strokes to complete the course." That didn't sound too difficult.

The Great One gave Yuri his assignment on Sunday, which was fortunate since there was a golf tournament on Yuri's wide-screen plasma TV that afternoon. He carefully observed the professional golfers as they boomed three-hundred-yard drives and hit soaring pitch shots that spun backwards toward the hole after they landed. He watched as they spent huge amounts of time studying the flawless surface of the green before smoothly stroking their ball into the hole. The announcers made it all sound highly dramatic and extremely difficult, but Yuri noticed that none of the lithe young men were sweating as they played, so how difficult could it be?

The only somewhat confusing part of the game was the equipment. According to what Yuri saw during the telecast, he needed a surprisingly large number of implements and accoutrements for such a simple game. He had to have golf clubs, of course, but also bags, shoes, gloves, shirts, hats, and special pants as well. Not to mention balls, all of which needed to go farther, fly straighter, and land softer, according to the commercials. It was a good thing Yuri received an unsolicited credit card in the mail every day.

Monday morning, he looked in the yellow pages and found a nearby golf shop located at a driving range that advertised itself as the place to "conquer par," which was very convenient for Yuri's purposes. Yuri drove there immediately and filled the trunk of his car with clubs and many other essential items the smiling salesman said he needed, including some that Yuri had not seen on television, like a full-body rain suit and an ionizing club cleaner. The helpful clerk also suggested Yuri take along several books and magazines to help him learn the game. The only thing Yuri didn't buy was an electronic range finder, since the multi-scan lens in his right eye and the micro-chip embedded behind it made the implement superfluous. The store owner gave both Yuri and the salesman a big hug when the credit card machine blinked its approval of the transaction. Yuri was armed and ready.

The next day at the driving range, Yuri turned up his nose at the scuffed, obviously pre-owned balls the other players were using. As he casually unwrapped one of the boxes of shiny new golf balls he had bought the day before, he ignored the stares of the other golfers. He thought they were probably just jealous of his fine equipment. He also surmised they must need a lot of practice, since their rusty buckets held hundreds of balls that they hit one after another in rapid fire. Yuri figured he would just hit the three balls in the little package first and save the other nine in the box for another time.

Yuri set the first ball on the plastic tee embedded in the green rubber mat and took the largest club, the driver, out of his bag. He swung it around a few times. It felt great! The cantaloupe-sized club head gave him confidence and he loved the swooshing sound it made as he swept it through the air, although the golfer in the next stall didn't like it much when the club's head cover went zooming past his ear. Yuri resolved to remove it before he swung the club next time.

He stepped up to the ball as he had seen the men on TV do, swung as hard as he could, and looked out into the distance to watch the ball fly into the sky. Except it didn't. After searching the horizon for several moments, Yuri realized that the ball had not moved from its perch on the plastic tee in front of him. Strange, he thought. Maybe I didn't swing hard enough. He took a death grip on the big club's handle, clenched his jaw in determination, and swung again as hard as he could. Whack-WHAP! The ball smacked into the wooden partition between Yuri and the now-terrified man in the next stall who had dodged the head cover. Where the ball went after that, Yuri didn't see, so he took another one out of the little package and placed it on the tee. Maybe this game isn't quite as easy as it looks, he thought. He ignored the man in the next stall, who was muttering nasty words while he gathered up his belongings to move out of the line of fire.

WHOOSH! WHIFF! Whack-WHAP! KerPLOwee! Yuri swung several times before he finally hit one of the infuriating little white balls and saw it sail off into the air. The ball followed a very fancy curving path to the right, which Yuri watched with satisfaction, noting that his ball's flight path matched that of the other golfers at the range. He congratulated himself on mastering the first shot of the game so quickly and moved on to the next.

The players on TV, he remembered, used one of the small-headed clubs after they hit the big one, so he replaced the driver in his bag and pulled out one of the others. It must be a special club, he thought, since it was marked "S." Or, as he discovered when he held the club out, the "S" could simply mean "short," which it certainly was. In fact, the club was so short that Yuri couldn't reach the ball with it unless he bent over into an unnatural posture. He tried getting on his knees to hit the ball, but then the club was too long and, besides, several of the other golfers ran for cover when he took his warm-up swing from that position. Finally, Yuri got to his feet and gave up trying to use the club as it was. Grasping the head in one hand and the grip in the other, he stretched the steel shaft until the club was the appropriate length. As he addressed the ball, Yuri noticed that all the other golfers at the range had disappeared into the pro shop, except for one man who had fainted three stalls away. He must not be much of an athlete, Yuri thought, if he can't endure what little exertion this game required.

Yuri swung the "S" club hard at the ball. THUNK! went the club as it dug a long gouge in the hard rubber mat six inches behind the ball. The club's now-thin shaft snapped, sending the club head flying out across the turf. That must be why the salesman in the golf shop sold me so many extra clubs, Yuri thought.

Since he had learned one shot, Yuri decided he had practiced enough for one day. He packed his clubs in the huge golf bag the salesman had assured him was the best ("A fellow like you deserves nothing less than a Tour bag," he had said) and patiently put the unused balls back in their little boxes. As he approached the parking lot, the other golfers jumped in their cars and sped away, undoubtedly abashed at how poorly they had performed in comparison to Yuri.

Wednesday, Yuri reported to the Great One on his trans-galactic cell phone, keeping the conversation short because the roaming charges were outrageous. The Great One was pleased that Yuri had learned the first shot so rapidly but was not happy to hear about the other patrons at the driving range. "You must blend in, Corporal Glnstrxmlpghyq," he said. "If the earthlings suspect you are not one of them, your mission will be compromised." He paused for effect. "Remember your privileges and what will happen to them if you fail." Yuri promised to become a mere face in the crowd. "A face that shoots par, just like everyone else," the Great One reminded him.

Yuri devoted the rest of that day to studying the golf books and magazines he had bought at the golf shop. He was impressed with their scientific rigor and could see why he had not performed quite as well as he had expected at the driving range. He also discovered that the elaborately curving shot he had mastered was something to be avoided, not sought after, which explained why the other golfers who hit it that way wore such grim, defeated expressions as they pounded ball after ball into the air. That shot was called a "slice" or "banana ball" and page after page of every magazine was devoted to eradicating the innumerable swing flaws that caused it. Privately, Yuri thought the slice was probably the result of an evolutionary genetic defect in Earthling golfers, but he still spent the rest of the day studying stop-action photographs, pouring over complex diagrams with multi-colored circles, arrows, and algebraic symbols, and memorizing the "Twelve Keys To Straight Drives" along with the magazines' many other intricate and sometimes contradictory instructions. That evening, just to be safe, he ordered a Swingfix Balanceator he saw advertised on the Golf Channel, paying extra for rush delivery so it would arrive in twenty-four hours. Fuzzy Zoeller, an accomplished golfer and very cheerful fellow with monstrous bags under his eyes (a sign of wisdom on Yuri's home planet) repeatedly assured Yuri and the other viewers at two AM that the device would not only cure his slice but make him the envy of other golfers—just like Fuzzy himself.

The marvelous invention arrived Thursday as promised. It didn't take Yuri long to scan the assembly booklet and put the machine together in his living room, although he was a little baffled by the purpose of some of the smaller pieces, so he just left them off. As soon as the apparatus was erected, Yuri slipped the instructional video into the player in his wide-screen plasma TV and carefully followed the directions given by the instructor on the screen. He began by standing on a short platform balanced on a roller so that it see-sawed up and down depending on how Yuri shifted his weight. A long strap stretched from the platform to a band around Yuri's forehead to hold his head still. Another strap linked his elbows in front of his body and forced his hands into grooves molded into the specially-weighted practice club.

Yuri followed the teacher carefully, taking little baby swings as he learned to keep his balance on the rocking platform. As he grew bolder, he took longer and longer swings, marveling at the ease with which he was picking up the technique. The instructor on the video finally said to take a full swing, so Yuri wound up like a clock spring and let 'er rip. Unfortunately, one of the unused pieces Yuri thought was superfluous was the safety catch for the head strap, which allowed it to release so the player could complete his follow through. Yuri's right arm, propelled by the specially weighted practice club, caught the head strap and violently snapped his neck around with it, yanking his body to the left side of the platform and pitching him sideways onto the floor. The heavy practice club flew out of his hands and smashed into the wide-screen plasma TV.

Friday morning, Yuri awoke with a sore neck and a premonition that he had only twenty-four hours to live. Then he remembered a sign at the driving range advertising golf lessons, which made him feel better about his prospects for passing his test and surviving to collect his retirement pay. He loaded all his gear into the car, including the pile of tangled straps and shattered plywood that the Swingfix Balanceator had become, and drove to the range.

Yuri explained to the instructor that he needed a lesson to make sure he shot par tomorrow. The pro looked at him carefully to see if this was some sort of practical joke, decided Yuri was serious, and told him to leave the Swingfix Balanceator in the car. "Let me see you hit a few balls," he said, handing Yuri a seven iron. Yuri took a couple of warm-up swings, then slashed at the ball with all of his might. The leading edge of the club nicked the ball, which dribbled sadly onto the turf.

The teacher adjusted the position of Yuri's hands and told him to hit another ball. This one skittered across the grass for a few yards, never rising more than six inches above the surface. The teacher then told Yuri to hold his left arm straight and his head still, keep his weight between his feet, and turn his shoulders ninety degrees while turning his hips forty-five. Concentrating hard, Yuri sent the ball on a beautiful flight high into the air and onto the target green in the middle of the range. "Very good!" the teacher said while Yuri beamed. "Now do it again."

Yuri didn't see the point of that, since he had already obviously learned to make this shot, but, to humor the teacher (who mumbled something about a blind pig finding an acorn), he put another ball on the practice tee and swung extra hard. WHACK-crunch! YEOW! Yuri shanked the ball sideways into the teacher's leg, sending the poor man screaming to the ground clutching his knee. The lesson was apparently over, so Yuri went home.

Yuri waited until after five o'clock so he could use the weekend minutes on his trans-galactic phone plan, then called the Great One to report on his progress. "The game of golf isn't as easy as I initially thought, but I've mastered the two basic strokes," he said. Yuri described the perfect seven iron he had hit that morning during his lesson, leaving out the part about crippling the teacher.

"That sounds promising, Corporal Glnstrxmlpghyq," the Great One intoned. "I hope you will pass the test tomorrow." The Great One was well-known for giving such stirring motivational speeches to his men. The rousing words rang in Yuri's ears that night as he slept peacefully, dreaming of perfectly-struck golf balls sailing into the vast dark reaches of the universe.

The next morning, on the first tee of Centurion Hills Golf Course, Yuri introduced himself to the three other players in his group, making an extra effort to blend in as one of the guys by encouraging them all to shoot par like he was going to do. At first the men looked a little bemused, but it must have worked because they insisted Yuri hit first. He pulled the big driver out of the bag and, remembering to take off the head cover, swung it confidently a few times to loosen up his shoulders. Then he bent to put his ball on the white plastic tee like he had at the driving range, but there didn't seem to be one embedded in the grass. One of the men asked him what he was looking for and Yuri mumbled something about a tee, so the man gave him one from his pocket. It was different from the one at the range, but Yuri's advanced intelligence enabled him to immediately grasp the new concept. Holding the ball firmly in one hand, he drove the point of the tee firmly into it with the other, then stood the tee up on the ground with the ball impaled on its tip. It was a little wobbly, but it worked. Yuri noted with pleasure that the other men gasped in admiration.

Yuri hit a screaming drive that curved sharply into the trees about half way to the green. "Darn banana ball," he said, trying to sound like a regular guy as he stood aside to let the other men hit. They stepped carefully around him and hit their drives, none of which went as far as Yuri's, although all three were in the fairway. Yuri lifted his golf bag to his chest and walked toward the woods. He noticed that the other men carried their bags using the straps over their shoulders and were looking at him peculiarly, so he swung his around like theirs and laughed, hoping they would think he was just joking. The other golfers laughed along with him, although a little uneasily. Yuri congratulated himself on becoming one of the group so quickly.

It took several minutes, but Yuri finally found his ball beneath a bush. He tried to hit it, but the branches were in the way, so he took one of the short clubs and hacked away until he could reach the ball. THWACK! WHAP! His ball caromed off a tree and came to rest in a pile of twigs. CRASH! CRACK! He hit it into another tree. SMACK! WHACK! SPLAT! It ricocheted into a mud puddle. Yuri kept slashing away until he managed to get his ball out of the woods and onto the green. By the time he got there, he had struck the ball seventy times. It wasn't in the hole yet, but Yuri was undaunted. Par for this course was seventy-two and all he had to do was roll the ball across the smooth surface of the green, up a little hill, and knock it into the hole about twelve feet away.

The other men in the group waited nervously for him to putt. Yuri walked back and forth several times like the golfers on TV. He squatted down three times and cupped his hands around the visor of his golf cap. He didn't know why he was doing any of these things, of course, but enjoyed them none the less. Finally, he selected a club he hadn't used yet, the lob wedge, and stepped up to the ball. The club was marked "L" and Yuri assumed that meant it would hit the ball "low." He didn't swing hard, since he was only a few feet away, but the club scooped out a surprisingly long strip of the carpet-like turf before it launched the ball almost straight up into the air. The club must have been mislabeled, Yuri thought. Somehow, the ball came to rest three feet from the hole.

Yuri expected his playing partners to applaud such a shot, but they had dropped their golf bags and were running toward the club house. He thought their behavior was odd, but then he realized the sky had darkened as if there were a total eclipse. Yuri looked up and saw the Great One's star cruiser hovering above the green, blocking out the sun. It looked vaguely like a golf cart the size of a football field. The sight made Yuri a little queasy, too.

"Par is no longer mathematically possible, Corporal Glnstrxmlpghyq," the Great One's voice sounded from above. Yuri was confused.

"But par is seventy-two—and I only have this one very small stroke to make!" he stammered.

"That will not leave you any strokes to make on the other holes, Corporal," the Great One explained. "Par is for all eighteen holes on the course, not just the first one."

Comprehension dawned in Yuri's golf-fogged brain. No wonder the game had seemed to simple! Yuri had become confused by the TV announcers' references to par for the course and par for the hole and birdies and bogies and up-and-downs and greens in regulation and all the other techno-golfibberish they spouted. "But that's not fair," Yuri protested.

"Dare you question the rules of golf!" the voice roared from above. "Golf is an eminently fair game, Corporal, but like life, it is sometimes also unpleasant." Yuri trembled and the voice softened. Magnanimously, the Great One asked, "Would you like to finish the hole before your privileges are revoked?"

Yuri swallowed, then nodded vaguely. The star cruiser bobbed up and down in the slight breeze that wafted across the course. Sirens wailed in the distance. Yuri sighed. He had not been treated fairly, but he knew that further argument would be in vain. He considered his options, neither of which were appealing and both of which—putting out or just picking up his ball—would end in a cloud of Yuri-matter blasted into the universe as atom-sized particles.

He decided to go ahead and play. Yrui looked at the "L" club in his hands, wondering if it would be appropriate for the final golf stroke in his too-short life. Then he visualized the last shot he hit with that club and a third option occurred to him.

"Are you going to putt or what?" the Great One growled.

"Yes sir," Yuri answered. "I was just enjoying the last of my privileges." Yuri bent over the ball and gripped the club tightly. He didn't even glance at the hole three feet away, but instead looked up once into the sky, as if in prayer, and adjusted his stance slightly. Concentrate, Yuri, concentrate, he told himself. He took a full, slow backswing, accelerated down and through the ball, and took a perfect divot out of the green. The ball flew straight up just like last time, though, and Yuri craned his neck to follow its flight. It climbed like a rocket straight into the sky and directly toward the four-inch-wide proton-intake tube on the bottom of the Great One's star cruiser, where it was sucked inside with a loud PFLOOP! The star cruiser shimmered, then shook violently for a few seconds before it exploded into a million billion points of light that twinkled away into the perfect cerulean sky over the golf course.

Yuri blinked. He picked up his clubs and walked to the second tee, determined more than ever to shoot par.

Dave Donelson

Screaming Blue Yips

Lenny didn't see the little blue gnome until he got to the sixth green. He didn't believe his eyes, of course. Would you? But there it was, as big—or as small—as life, kneeling behind Lenny's ball and lining up the thirty-footer just like a PGA tour caddie.

Lenny walked up the hill onto the elevated green and yelled "Hey!" He didn't know what else to do, never having encountered a gnome on the golf course before. But the blue gnome didn't pay any attention. He just kept examining the line of the putt, tilting his head first one way and then the other, leaning forward, then back on his heels, shading his eyes with his little blue fingers.

"Hey what!" shouted back Jimbo, one of the Lenny's playing partners. The third man in the group, Bruce, was busy lining up his own putt and just looked irritated. Lenny didn't pay any attention to Jimbo or to Bruce's expression. The man was born looking irritated. Lenny had other matters to attend to, like the blue gnome now doing a Camilo Villegas Spiderman imitation behind his ball.

"Get away from that ball!" Lenny shouted. The blue gnome stood and scowled at Lenny, who got a good look at it as he walked closer. Its skin was a fine shade of cerulean blue, which contrasted nicely with its flaming orange eyebrows and ragged goatee. The gnome wore pointy yellow shoes with curled-up toes, red-and-white striped hose, a jerkin that was half gold and half purple, and a green pointed hat with a white feather in the brim. Even by the standards of golf couture, the gnome was dressed funny.

The gnome stepped around Lenny's ball and pointed to a small brown spot on the green two-thirds of the way to the hole. Apparently, it was giving Lenny the line.

"Get out of here!" Lenny shouted again and vigorously tried to wave the gnome away. The gnome's orange eyebrows drew together and its eyes narrowed as it traced a sweeping line in the air from Lenny's ball, through the brown spot, and to the cup with a crooked blue forefinger. It stuck its hands on its hips and squinted meaningfully at Lenny.

"Who are you yelling at?" Jimbo asked.

Lenny pointed at the little blue gnome. "That little guy standing right there!" he replied.

"Guy? What guy?" Jimbo replied, naturally enough, since he didn't see anybody on the green except Lenny and Bruce, who was now checking his line from the other side of the hole and scowling, which was his normal expression when he wasn't irritated.

"There's a little blue guy standing right there. Don't you see him?" Lenny asked. He jabbed toward the blue gnome with his putter. "A little blue guy dressed in funny clothes!"

At that, the gnome bared his teeth in a soundless snarl and stomped his foot in the line of Lenny's putt. "Hey! Cut that out!" Lenny yelled. He couldn't believe what the little jerk had just done to his line. The gnome scuttled over to the cup and defiantly dug his heel into the grass in front of the hole. Then he stuck his tongue out at Lenny and disappeared. His tongue was blue, too.

"Up yours, buddy," Lenny shouted at the spot where the gnome had vanished.

"Would you hold it down?" Bruce demanded. "I'm trying to make a putt here." Lenny stood and stared at the place where the blue gnome had been while Bruce stroked his putt from the far side of the green. It was an excellent lag putt that stopped less than a foot from the hole.

"That's good," Jimbo said. He looked at Lenny, who stood motionless next to his ball staring into space. "Are you going to putt, or what?" he said.

Lenny wiped his hand across his eyes and snapped himself back to reality. "Uh, yeah. Sure," he muttered. He crouched over his ball and slapped it in the general direction of the hole. The ball bounced through the gnome's footprint but managed to stay more or less on line right up to the hole, when it hit the heel mark and hopped hard to the left, missing the cup by a good two inches. "See what that son of a bitch did?" he demanded, glaring at the ball.

"You shouldn't call your ball names, you know," Bruce said. "It's bad luck."

"But that little bastard in the goofy clothes stomped all over my line!" Lenny protested. Jimbo looked at Bruce and grinned. Bruce grimaced, which for him was a grin.

"Riiight," Jimbo said.

"Pick it up," Bruce added. "It's good." Lenny snatched up his ball and stormed off the green.

* * *

Shaken by the missed putt, not to the mention his encounter with the blue gnome, Lenny hit a snap hook from the seventh tee into the left rough. He lucked out with a good lie, though, and came back with a magnificent recovery shot that left him in the fairway just a few yards short. He chipped to within three feet of the hole and was feeling pretty good about par as he strode onto the green. Until he saw the little blue gnome kneeling once again behind his ball.

Lenny looked around frantically for his partners, but Jimbo was in a huge trap to the left of the green and Bruce was busy advising him on how to get out. Lenny hurried toward his ball and the blue gnome scampered around to the hole, where he bent over and pointed a crooked blue finger at a spot an inch to the right of the cup. He smiled encouragingly at Lenny.

"Get out of here!" Lenny snarled as he marked his ball. The gnome frowned and stabbed his blue finger emphatically at the spot again. Just then, Jimbo's ball exploded out of the sand and rolled up just behind Lenny's mark.

"Do you see that?" Lenny demanded as Jimbo climbed exultantly out of the trap.

"Yeah, boy! Some shot, huh?" Jimbo answered.

"No! I mean the little blue guy over there." Lenny pointed toward the hole. The gnome glared at him and growled just before he vanished again.

"Another little blue guy?" Jimbo chuckled, "or the same one as the last hole?"

"Never mind," Lenny snapped.

Bruce sank his twelve footer for par and Jimbo rammed his own putt into the hole right after it. Lenny replaced his ball on the mark and knelt behind it to check the line. The little blue gnome re-appeared behind the hole. He scowled at Lenny and pointed to the spot just outside the cup on the right.

"Get away from there!" Lenny shouted.

"Chill out, would you?" Jimbo said.

"It's that little blue guy again! Don't you see him?!"

Bruce asked with disgust, "For chrissakes, Lenny, how many Bloody Mary's did you drink for breakfast?"

"You really ought to stop at two when you're going to play," Jimbo added.

"Screw you!" Lenny answered. "And screw you, too," he snarled at the gnome, who flipped him a blue digit and disappeared.

"Well, putt the ball, would you?" Jimbo said.

"Yeah. That's not a gimmee no matter how many little green men you see," Bruce grinned.

"He's blue, dammit," Lenny said between clenched teeth. He drew back his putter and tried to ram the ball home like Jimbo had done, but it ran two feet past instead, although it did pass over the spot where the gnome told him to aim. "Damn!" Lenny said.

* * *

The eighth hole isn't much of a hole, a par three 172 downhill, with a big two-tiered green protected ineffectually by a couple of middling bunkers on either side. Lenny's nerves were so jangled, though, that he chunked his tee shot. His ball landed thirty-five yards short of the green. He chili-dipped an easy pitch, too, leaving a long putt from the apron across the first tier and up the ridge to the hole cut on the second level. He would be lucky to three-putt from there and he knew it. His disposition didn't improve when the little blue gnome appeared immediately in front of him as he stood behind his ball eyeing the impossible putt.

"Get out of my line!" Lenny growled. The gnome held up his left hand like a traffic cop, then pointed across the green with his right. "Beat it, you little creep!" Lenny yelled.

"Enough already with the little green men!" Jimbo called to him from where he was marking his ball on the second tier. Lenny ignored him.

The gnome danced a little blue jig, then extended his arms, one purple, one gold, like wings. He raised his bushy orange eyebrows in wide-eyed insistence until he had Lenny's full attention, then trotted across the green like a kid playing airplane to a spot on the crest of the second tier. There he turned and flew to the hole. Along the way, he passed within two feet of Bruce, who was crouching behind his ball concentrating on the line for his birdie putt. Bruce didn't even blink.

Lenny yelled, "Get away from there!" The gnome straddled the hole and jabbed a blue finger down toward it excitedly.

"Screw you!" Bruce yelled back, since he thought Lenny was yelling at him.

"No! I . . . Oh, never mind," Lenny answered. He tried to shut the little blue gnome out of his mind and pick a line for his putt. "Doesn't matter, I'll be lucky to get it within ten feet," he muttered to himself. Out of the corner of his eye, he saw the gnome dancing his jig on the crest of the ridge where he wanted him to aim. Instead, Lenny chose a spot well to the right. He took a big sweeping stroke and his ball skittered across the first tier, up the incline, and turned left before coming to rest still twenty feet from the hole. The gnome jumped up and down, ripped his green pointed hat off his head, and slammed it into the ground in frustration at Lenny's refusal to take his advice.

"I'm not seeing this," Lenny said to himself as he trudged to his ball. "I've got to get a grip." He didn't bother to check his line this time, but just stepped up to the ball and aimed vaguely at the hole. The blue gnome rushed over and jumped right in front of his ball, though, as if trying to prevent him from touching it.

"Get away!" Lenny screamed.

"You're NOT away! I am!" Jimbo shouted from the other side of the green. Lenny stepped back, confused, while the gnome leered at him. "Sheesh!" Jimbo said as he bent over his putt. The blue gnome put a finger to his lips signaling Lenny to be quiet while Jimbo putted. Infuriated, Lenny waited until Jimbo's ball was on its way, then took a backhanded swipe at the gnome with his putter. The gnome jumped out of the way and shook his blue fist violently in the air. Jimbo's ball rattled into the cup and Lenny's head snapped around at his triumphant yell. When he looked back, the gnome was gone.

"I must be losing my mind," Lenny thought as he tried to compose himself over the ball. He shook his head to clear it, then stroked the putt to within two feet. "That's good, isn't it?" he asked.

"Not the way you've been putting," Bruce answered. Lenny gritted his teeth and took his stance over the ball. He made a smooth stroke, but just an instant before he made contact with the ball, the pointed toe of a yellow shoe reached in and deflected the putter. The ball missed the cup by six inches and Lenny screamed in anguish. The gnome skipped out of reach, thumbed his blue nose at Lenny, and disappeared.

"You're a little yippy there, Lenny-boy," Jimbo observed. Lenny screamed again, so Bruce told him his come-backer was good.

* * *

Lenny muttered to himself all the way to the ninth tee, stopping only when Bruce gave him a dirty look and asked for quiet so he could tee off. After Bruce and Jimbo hit, Lenny stepped up. His hands shook so badly he could barely get the tee into the ground. Sweat ran into his eyes as he took his stance and tried to focus on the ball. He swung weakly and watched his ball dribble onto the ladies' tee. He whimpered.

Sympathetically, Jimbo said, "Relax, buddy. That's okay! Take a mulligan." Bruce nodded. Lenny grabbed the towel off his bag and mopped his face, trying to settle down. Then he took a deep breath and took another swing. The ball limped down the fairway. At least I got it past the ladies' tee, he thought. Jimbo chuckled and patted him consolingly on the shoulder as they walked off the tee.

The little blue gnome was not in sight when Lenny finally reached the green. He looked everywhere, whirling around unexpectedly a couple of times to try to catch him off guard, but the gnome was nowhere to be seen. Lenny could feel Jimbo watching him out of the corner of his eye while Bruce practically tiptoed around to his ball. They think I'm nuts, Lenny thought, and maybe they're right. He looked around again just to be sure the coast was clear before he marked his ball.

All went well while first Bruce and then Jimbo putted out. Lenny looked casually around the green, but saw no sign of any gnomes, blue or otherwise. He re-checked the line of his easy twelve-footer and saw a small white feather near the hole. Something bothered him about it, but he shook off the feeling as he walked up and flicked it away. Just a touch

22

of the heebie-jeebies, he thought. Still, the white feather tickled a corner of his mind as he bent over his putt. He straightened back up and took a deep, mind-cleansing breath. Jimbo started to say something, then thought better of it and kept his mouth shut. Lenny leaned back over the ball, steadied his eyes on it, and stroked it toward the hole. It rolled true for the first eight feet, then veered slightly to the right for no apparent reason, coming to rest still two feet short of the cup.

"I know, I know," Lenny said, shaking his head. "It's not a gimmee." He stepped up to the ball and marked it, trying to get back into some semblance of his pre-putt routine. As he set the ball back down carefully in front of the mark, he remembered where he had seen the little white feather. It was stuck in the gnome's stupid green hat! Lenny's vision blurred as he realized that the gnome was still stalking him. He was here, somewhere! Lenny stood up so quickly the blood rushed from his head and he staggered a little.

"You okay?" Jimbo asked. Lenny didn't answer. His eyes twitched from side to side looking everywhere for his little blue nemesis. He whirled around once, then back again, then yet again to face Bruce and Jimbo.

"You keep a lookout!" he ordered.

Startled, they took a step backward. Bruce whispered, "You throw the net on him and I'll run for help." Jimbo snorted.

Lenny turned back to his putt, whipping his head back and forth in search of the gnome. "I can do this," he muttered. He had no feeling in his hands and arms as he bent over the ball. Sweat ran into his eyes. The putter trembled as he drew it back and started his stroke in extreme slow motion.

Just as the putter face kissed the ball, a crooked blue finger jabbed his hand. Lenny's ball shot past the hole. He roared and turned, swinging his putter wildly at something only he could see. The gnome danced out of the way and stuck his thumbs in his ears, flapping his fingers. Lenny bellowed and, swinging his putter like a baseball bat, ran at him with death in his eyes. The gnome turned and fled laughing and taunting across the green, through a bunker, and into the woods. Lenny darted after him, his cries of frustration and rage echoing through the trees as he disappeared.

Eyes wide in wonderment, Jimbo looked at Bruce. Bruce just shook his head and said, "He really needs to do something about those yips."

Grand Slam

It was a dark and moonless night. Stormy, too, but you couldn't prove it by Eddie Monk, who sat glued to the computer screen in the middle of the newsroom miles away from the nearest window trying to turn the incoherent garbage filed by Dan Stacey into six inches of readable copy for the first edition of the *NY Herald*. He had three minutes.

The reporter's story wasn't complicated—a simple recap of the locker room gripe session after a grinding season-opener loss by the Mets—but Stacey had managed to bury the lead yet again. As the clock ticked, Monk finally found it in the fourth paragraph. He cut and pasted it to the top of the story, wrote a six-word transition for the next paragraph, hit the send button, and he was done for the night with a full minute to spare. Who said a night editor's work was never done? It was two AM and now that the paper was put to bed, Monk could grab some shuteye, too. He had a ten o'clock tee time reserved, so he had just enough time to drive home, catch five or so hours of sleep, and make it to the range to warm up before stepping onto the first tee.

Monk threw on his jacket and checked as he did every night to make sure his pen was in his pocket. Other writers might scribble their way through life with just any old ballpoint, but Monk's was a sterling silver pen awarded by the International Golf Writers Association in recognition of his twenty-five years covering the game. The closer Monk came to retirement, the more he treasured it. He would make good use of the pen when he started working on the *Herald's* coverage of the Masters this week. If the owners of the *NY Herald* had their way—and they always did—this year's would be his last. He tried not to think about that, but it was a hard subject to avoid.

It's time, Editor-in-chief Charlie Stogel had said when he called Monk into his office on January 2. "You've done great work and all that, but the new computer system is going to mean lighter workloads for all the editors. And free online readership cuts into revenues something fierce—you know the story. I hate to do this, Monk, but I strongly urge you to retire."

"And if I don't?" Monk asked.

"The union contract says I can't force you—you know that. But I can eliminate your job. You've got enough seniority to stay on the payroll for another year or two, but you would end up on the day shift, probably doing lifestyle feature crap."

"No sports? No nights?"

"No sports. No nights. Sorry, Monk."

As he had done ever since, Monk drove home along the Hutchinson River Parkway trying to decide what to do. He wasn't old enough to retire, at least in his own mind, yet he sure didn't want to end his career writing about doggie day care and the latest, greatest exhibit at the Central Park Zoo. And he really, really didn't want to work during the day. His night shift hours enabled him to play golf almost every day, which he did when the weather allowed. His handicap hovered around ten and he had no delusions about ever getting much better, but that was fine as long as he was healthy enough to keep playing. When he retired—when he was damned good and ready to retire, thank you very much—he planned to move someplace south where he could get a part time job as a ranger or starter on a course to supplement his pension and play golf year 'round. He had his eye on The Dunes in Myrtle Beach, but he wouldn't have enough saved to get a membership if he retired this year.

What's more, Monk knew he would miss covering the professional game when he retired. He'd been glad to give up the grinding travel and repetitive press conferences of the PGA beat in favor of a night editor's position a few years ago, but he still shaped the paper's coverage of the Tour, giving a guiding hand to Sully, the reporter who had replaced him, and contributing features and sidebars to round out the coverage, especially of the majors. On the other hand, Monk thought as he pulled into his driveway, it would almost be worthwhile to end his career writing about the biggest story in golf, which could happen this year.

Monk knew it was a long, long shot, but it was possible that someone could win the Grand Slam this season. No one had accomplished the feat since Bobby Jones set the bar in 1930 by winning the four biggest titles of the day, the U.S. and British Open and Amateur Championships. As the game evolved, two premier professional events, the Masters and the PGA Championship, replaced the amateur events in the press-created series, but no one had ever again achieved the mark of winning all four in the same year. Ben Hogan came closest in 1953, but the state of transatlantic travel of the time meant he couldn't get across the pond from the British Open to the PGA Championship in time to compete. Tiger Woods had once held all four trophies at the same time, but that didn't count in Monk's mind—or anybody else's except

Tiger's—since the wins were consecutive but spread over two years. It was a great accomplishment, but it was no Grand Slam.

Everyone had pretty much given up on Tiger's chances of winning a legitimate slam, but there was a lot of talk this year about a German pro, Harold Lanack, who came out of nowhere two years ago to make a big splash on the tour. Monk wasn't convinced this was his year, but he was secretly rooting for him.

When he got back to the newsroom the next night, Monk started researching a color piece about Lanack to go with Sully's coverage of the Masters in Thursday's edition. There wasn't much to work with, but Monk thought he could build a story around why Lanack's game suddenly went from mediocre to world-beating. Solving a mystery always makes a good hook for a feature story. The problem was, Monk couldn't find anything to hang on his hook.

Harold Lanack was a marginal player on the European PGA Tour with dozens of missed cuts to his credit until two years ago. Then he won a relatively unknown tournament in Austria, which got him into the British Open for the first time. He managed to make it to the weekend at Royal St. Anne's, but that was about it. For reasons known only to the PGA of America (Monk suspected they were under pressure from the PGA Tour to fatten the field with beatable Europeans so an American player would stand a better chance of winning), Lanack's single win got him a special invitation to play in the PGA Championship at Whistling Straits. In a tale straight from the Brothers Grimm, Lanack came from nowhere to win the Wannamaker trophy.

By itself, that victory, now almost two years old, wouldn't have generated any speculation about Lanack's potential for a Grand Slam. In fact, it would have been true-to-form for him to join the long list of one-major winners that constitute little more than footnotes in the game's record books and who end their careers making personal appearances and running restaurant/bars/golf courses with their names on them. Last year, though, Lanack leapt onto the scene with both feet. He won four of the fifteen tournaments he entered, including the U.S. Open at the Olympic Club in San Francisco. Suddenly, Harold Lanack was The Next Big Thing.

Lanack even had a nickname, "Harry The Closer," hung on him by a headline writer for the *NY Post*. He had earned it by turning in his best score of the week on Sunday every time he won. In fact, Lanack had never gone into a final round better than tied for the lead. Both of his major wins were by single strokes. He had come from five strokes behind at Whistling Straits and an incredible seven back to win the U.S. Open at Olympic.

Monk wrote about Lanack's major wins but he couldn't find much else about the man to make a story. Finally, he saw something in Lanack's record that no one else seemed to have noticed. It wasn't much of a hook, but it was worth noting. Harry The Closer had no near-wins. In fact, when Monk examined the tournament records for last year, he found that Lanack either won by a whisker or missed by a mile. In the eleven tournaments he didn't win, he never finished in the top half of the field—and in five of them he missed the cut. Reluctantly, Monk decided that the golf world had crowned the Grand Slam king a bit prematurely.

That week, the Masters looked to be more of the same. Lanack started poorly on Thursday, had a better Friday, and finished Saturday four strokes behind the leader, Ernie Els, who was making a late-career bid to add a green jacket to his wardrobe. But before Lanack could begin his charge Sunday morning, a brutal murder overshadowed the drama on the leaderboard. The lone remaining feminine rights protester left from Martha Burke's fruitless effort to force August National to accept women members, a determined young woman named Clarice, was found dead in Augusta. Even the *Post* wouldn't run a picture of her eviscerated corpse draped over the card table she'd bravely—and vainly—manned all week in the vacant lot set aside for protesters a few blocks from Magnolia Drive.

The police activity tied up traffic, delaying the arrival of several players, but Augusta National Chairman Charles Morton Prendergast IV, aka "Tootie," simply moved the first tee time back an hour, told the Georgia State Police to get things under control, and informed CBS they should expect to miss broadcasting *Sixty Minutes* that night. As Sully pointed out when he called Monk with the story, Tootie never missed a tee time, including the one on his own wedding day.

The murder may not have stopped the Masters, but it played havoc with everyone's game. Everyone, that is, except Harry The Closer, who won with a tap-in birdie at number twelve, an eagle at fifteen, and a birdie putt on 16 that out-curled Tiger's slo-mo YouTube marvel. His drive on 18 was hit so hard, according to Sully, that his golf shoes "left claw marks on the turf."

Monk wasn't surprised when the murder in Augusta was crowded off the front page by the wire service photo of Lanack rushing into his caddie's arms on the eighteenth green. Monk noticed with a chuckle that Lanack badly needed a haircut—and maybe a shave. He sent an email to

Sully to check whether Lanack had some superstition about personal grooming during the majors the way some ball players didn't shave while playing the World Series. He also made a note to himself to see if there was a human interest story behind Lanack's caddie, Vlad Krajivek. Aside from the fact that he came with Lanack from Europe, nobody seemed to know anything about him.

Golf tournaments, even the majors, make headlines for a day at best, but Monk tried to use the flurry of interest in the potential Grand Slam to convince the powers-that-be that the paper needed him. He even proposed to travel with Harold Lanack to make sure the story got the in-depth coverage it deserved. He figured if he could make a big enough splash, he'd have a better chance of holding on to his job next year. Stogel didn't buy it.

"Harold Lanack could win the Kentucky Derby, Wimbledon, and climb Mount Everest backwards and it still won't save your job, Monk. Besides, I have enough trouble finding the budget to keep Sully on the road."

Monk didn't want to permanently put the cap on his pen, but he felt the time coming.

* * *

No one but Monk and a few diehard fans noticed that Harold Lanack faded into the background and disappeared after his win at Augusta. He didn't play at Harbour Town, although it is not unusual for the Masters winner to skip that event the following week, but he also dropped out of the next two tour events, too, which Monk thought was odd. Not unheard of, just odd.

But Lanack came back to the tour with a flourish four weeks after the Masters at the Tournament Players Championship. The PGA Tour liked to call the event at TPC Sawgrass the fifth major, but Monk, like most purists, considered it at best a near major. Granted, the field is almost always strong and the Pete Dye course is one of the toughest they play, but there was something about the circus atmosphere around the famous island green at the seventeenth hole that made the tournament a bit gimmicky for Monk's tastes. Goofy golf or not, Harry The Closer came from behind once again on Sunday to win the tournament despite having dunked his ball in the water on seventeen both Thursday and Friday.

Once again, though, the tournament was marred by an ugly death, although this one was ruled accidental and didn't make any of the papers except the *Jacksonville Times-Union*. According to the wire service story Monk read, a guest's body was found in the lake behind the Sawgrass Hotel Sunday morning by a maintenance crew. The police speculated he was trying to swim to the cute little fake island green that floats in the lake as a comic tribute to the seventeenth hole a few blocks away. The coroner reported the cause of death wasn't drowning, however, but rather an alligator bite to the throat. When Monk asked Sully what he'd heard about the incident, the reporter said the tongue-in-cheek rumor among the press corps was that Tiger's caddie had tracked the man down after he'd clicked a camera during the great one's backswing that day.

"Speaking of caddies," Monk said, "Did you find out anything about Vlad Krajivek?"

"Not much," Sully answered. "He lists his nationality as Austrian and his race as 'Roma,' whatever that is."

"That means he's a Gypsy, to use the politically incorrect term," Monk explained. "Anything else?"

"Nope. Nobody ever heard of him before he hooked up with Lanack at the Austrian Open. Apparently, Lanack didn't have a regular caddie before him. Probably couldn't afford one."

"Is that all you've got?"

"Sorry, Monk. The guy doesn't even hang around the other caddies. Doesn't talk much, either. Lanack's the same way. You never see either one of them alone. They're always together. Fluff Cowan said Lanack may be 'The Closer' but Krajivek stays so close to him he should be called 'The Keeper.' He swears one time he saw Krajivek walking Lanack on a leash."

"Oh for God's sake, Sully. Cut the comedy and give me something to work with here, would you?" The reporter laughed and said he'd get back to him.

The TPC win pushed Grand Slam fever up another notch, so Monk dug a little deeper into Lanack's background and started writing the story as if he'd already won. Covering an athlete setting a record is like writing an obituary—if you wait until it happens, it's too late to do the research.

Unfortunately, there just wasn't much more to find out about Harold Lanack. He was born in Munich, the middle child of a middle class couple of middle achievers. His father was a weekend golfer who introduced him to the game but didn't do anything else to help his career. Lanack squeaked onto the European tour on the cut line from Q

School, then spent the next eight years trying to hold on to his card. His big break was also his first come-from-behind Sunday win. It was at the Austrian Open at Diamond Country Club in Atzenbrugg, a tournament remarkable for absolutely nothing else.

Monk tried to interview Lanack, but got no response. He appealed to the PGA Tour press office, but they couldn't help, either. Monk could sense the frustration in the press aide's voice when he told him Lanack was refusing all interview requests while he prepared for the U.S. Open at Shinnecock.

Still trying to find a hook the Monday before the U.S. Open, Monk started trolling through the newspaper's morgue for coverage of Lanack's wins, hoping to snag an incident he could use to create a story angle. Between time spent rewriting the beat reporters' stories about the Mets and Yankees, he plowed through the files for the PGA Championship at Whistling Straits. He researched the usual databases with the expected parameters and came up with nothing new. When he expanded the search by filtering for stories about Kohler's American Club Resort during the tournament dates, all he found was an insipid travel review and a three paragraph story about the flock of black-faced sheep that browse the Irish Course, the sister course to Whistling Straits. Accordinging to a wire story, a dozen of them were killed that weekend. While some residents claimed it was the work of aliens, state police blamed coyotes. Frustrated, Monk threw his notes into the trash, stowed his pen in his pocket, and went home.

The next night, Monk delved into the databases looking for something—anything—from the U.S. Open at the Olympic Club the year before. The only factoid he found was that Lanack had almost missed his tee time on the final Sunday. A small kerfuffle arose when Krajivek drove into the club at top speed with minutes to spare while Lanack put on his golf shoes in the back seat. The duo grabbed Lanack's clubs out of the trunk and abandoned the courtesy car on the road near the first tee. The USGA slapped Lanack on the wrist and that was the end of it. Lanack's win wiped the incident from everyone's mind that day. When asked about it later, Lanack said they had both simply overslept after a big meal the night before in San Francisco.

Grasping at straws, Monk did an online search of the police reports for San Francisco that Saturday night, but found nothing but the death of a man outside a homeless shelter in the Tenderloin district, which was quite a distance from the Olympic Club and the hotel where Lanack stayed.

Still, something was wrong with Harold Lanack. Every reportorial instinct Monk possessed told him there were too many blanks in the backstory, too few details of his everyday life off the golf course. His official PGA biography was useless and even the tabloids were having trouble coming up with anything, although not for lack of trying. After Lanack won the Masters, the *National Observer* ran a photo of Vlad Krajivek cavorting nude on the lawn of Lanack's home with a giant dog in the moonlight, but it was hardly credible given that the headline on the opposite page was "Martian Imposter Wins Key Senate Race."

At least Monk didn't have to depend entirely on Sully to do all the digging at the U.S. Open. The tournament was at Shinnecock Hills in Southampton, a two-hour drive from Manhattan. Monk would be able to catch some morning and early afternoon play, hang out on the range, and nose around the locker room while still having time to get back to the newsroom to work his shift. He'd miss playing a couple of rounds himself, but he figured he'd have plenty of time to play when he retired, want to or not.

The *Herald* devoted plenty of ink to the U.S. Open since it was played in the New York market. Sully did several human interest stories about the players while Monk did a piece on the history of the event at Shinncock that detailed Corey Pavin's steel-nerved win in 1995. Sully also wrote a short filler about how weather—especially the wind— played a key factor on the links. Monk added a sidebar after checking with the *Herald's* weather editor, Marv Tobin, who told him a front would move through that weekend, possibly bringing light rains but certainly high tides and more wind than usual since the moon would be full Saturday night. Monk made a note to put rain gear in his car just in case.

Monk saw Harry the Closer in person for the first time on the practice tee Wednesday. Lanack had taken a place at the far left where a fence and low hill shielded him from spectators on two sides. His caddie kept watch on the other side to keep the reporters at bay. Most of the players were happy to chat with the press on the range, but Lanack obviously wasn't one of them. Monk worked his way through the reporters milling around and watched Lanack at work. His swing had the metronomic regularity that marks almost every tour pro's, but it was nothing special. He was a big, tall man, not lithe and lean like so many of the younger fitness fanatics on tour. Monk was particularly struck by Lanack's face, which had a strong, square jaw and thick lips that never smiled. His eyes were deep-sunk and dark beneath a prognathous brow with black, heavy eyebrows. During the fifteen minutes Monk watched, Lanack never cracked a smile or spoke—even to his caddie. He might win a Grand Slam, Monk thought, but he's not going to get his own show on the Golf Channel.

When he finished pounding balls, Lanack handed his club to Krajivek and stood quietly while the caddie hoisted his bag to his shoulder. As they walked away, Monk called out, "Harold! What about the Grand Slam? Think you'll make it?" Lanack didn't even turn his head. Several of the other reporters shouted questions, too, but Lanack and Krajivek completely ignored them. Monk noted with interest that none of the other pros said anything to Lanack as he walked by them on the range. Even Phil Mickelson, never at a loss for words, opened his mouth as they approached but apparently changed his mind and looked back down at his ball.

Lanack wasn't much more communicative during the fifteen minutes he was on stage at the pre-tournament press conference *cum* platitude parade. "I am honored to play in such august event," he said in a heavily-accented growl. "Shinnecock is very fine test of golf" and "The key to winning tournament will be keep ball in fairway" were among the other stock responses he made to the reporters' equally stock questions. Frustrated with the banality of it all, Monk racked his brain for a question that didn't have a standard answer. He remembered his conversation with Marv Tobin just as the U.S.GA press manager called for last question.

"How will the full moon affect your game this week?" Monk called out.

Lanack looked at his blankly. His heavy brow knotted for a moment as the question sank in. Finally he said, "That is stupid question" and left the room. Vlad Krajivek gave Monk a long, hard stare before following Lanack out the door.

"Full moon?" scoffed Scully as Monk stood up to the leave. "What the hell was that all about?"

"Just trying to see if the guy is human," Monk said.

"As opposed to what?"

"As opposed to just another automaton with PGA-programmed responses, that's what."

Sully smirked, "You should know better."

The next day, Lanack had a morning tee time so Monk followed him around Shinnecock and watched the German card a mediocre 73. His Friday round wasn't much better, but the blustery conditions Marv Tobin had predicted ruined most of the field's scores so Lanack stayed in contention. Monk noticed a distinct difference in Lanack's play Saturday. He seemed to drive the ball a bit farther and he missed very few putts. He ended the day tied for the lead with Mickelson.

Harry the Closer lived up to his name Sunday, although the day didn't start well for him. Mickelson pulled out to a two-stroke lead on the front nine and Monk was sure Lanack had hammered a nail into his coffin when he hit it long and left on the 160-yard par three eleventh hole. The green runs steeply away from that spot, but Lanack finessed a delicate chip that somehow found the hole for a birdie. He eagled the sixteenth hole by avoiding the twenty bunkers on the par five while hitting a perfect second shot to three feet below the hole. Mickelson blew his last chance on the final hole when he sliced a driver into the fescue in a desperate gamble for a winning birdie rather than playing a three wood for a safe par that would have sent the match into a playoff.

At the awards ceremony, Monk was close enough to Lanack to see his flushed cheeks—unshaven as usual—and severely bloodshot eyes. He wrote both off to the wind that whipped off the Atlantic, but wondered how Lanack could see to putt with eyes that looked like they were burning from the inside.

* * *

Harold Lanack's second major victory of the year stoked the fire under Grand Slam fever. The media laid it on thick in advance of the British Open. Carnoustie Golf Club hosted the tournament, so there was an endless stream of articles, TV clips, and radio talk shows comparing Harry the Closer with Jean Van de Velde, the poor Frenchman who suffered a crushing self-inflicted defeat when he blew a three-stroke lead on the final hole in 1999. Lanack, according to the pundits and talk show callers, was genetically incapable of playing that badly. Monk wouldn't go that far, but he wasn't about to bet against him.

It's a good thing he didn't, because Lanack won the Open by protecting a one-stroke lead over Rory McIlroy with a five iron off the tee at 18, a layup wedge to Barry Burn, and a sand wedge to two feet.

In the pandemonium, almost no one noticed that Colin Montgomerie's wife had reported him missing Sunday morning. His portly body was found in a gorse thicket not far from the course as the crowds filed out after Lanack collected the Claret Jug. Commentators speculated that Monty had been out walking in the full moon in a fit of inebriated despair at missing the cut on Friday. Official reports the next day said he was felled by food poisoning and his body was gnawed by stoats that scavenged around Barry Burn.

When Sully filed his final story from Scotland before flying home, he told Monk that the standard line in the press room was that Monty had gone for a walk and choked, something he did with regularity in the majors during his otherwise-outstanding career. "Personally," Sully added, "I think he's going to come back as a werewolf—full moon and all that—which will actually make him a kinder, gentler Monty."

"Very funny," Monk said, but his mind was elsewhere. The jokes about the full moon reminded him of something, but he couldn't put his finger on it.

While he was trying to figure it out, a news alert popped up on his computer screen. It was promoted by a scan term he'd forgotten to cancel, "Shinnecock." Monk started to delete the alert, then glanced at the headline: "Socialite Killed At U.S. Open Mansion." The brief story said that the body of a woman had been found in her Southampton mansion, which had been rented to a player in the U.S. Open at Shinnecock for the duration of the tournament. The vicious killing—the woman's throat was ripped out and her designer sweater shredded—must have taken place not long after the tournament since the body was four weeks old. It had lain undiscovered because the woman was believed to be travelling at the time. Her husband, a well-known Wall Street mogul, said he hadn't missed her for a month because he had been neck-deep in a merger and thought she was out of the country. "Muffy had some strange ideas," he was quoted, "But that's just one more thing I loved about her." He explained that she was supposed to be in Machu Pichu during U.S. Open week celebrating the summer solstice and observing the full moon.

That was it! Monk had been trying to remember what Marv Tobin had told him about Shinnecock—there was a full moon the Saturday of tournament week.

Monk had a crazy idea. He called the U.S.GA housing office and was told yes, Harold Lanack was indeed the renter where the murder occurred. Monk pulled up the PGA tour schedule on his computer screen and jotted a list of dates on a legal pad. Then he picked up the phone again.

"Marv, do you have some historical moon chart or something like that?"

"You mean a record of the phases of the moon?"

"Yes, I guess so," Monk said.

"Sure, what do you want to know?"

"Check these dates, would you?" Monk read off the Saturday dates during the Masters and the Tour Players Championship. "Where there full moons those nights?"

There was silence on the line while Tobin checked. "Yes," he said.

Monk was intrigued by cautious. "How about these?" He read off the dates for Whistling Straights and Olympic.

"Yep, you're on a roll," Tobin said.

Monk started to give Tobin some more dates, but the weather editor cut him off. "Look, Monk, I'm on deadline here. You don't need me to check for a full moon. Just pick one and count backwards or forwards by four weeks."

"Thanks!" Monk said. He hung up and quickly checked the rest of Lanack's wins. Every one of them had come on Sunday following a full moon.

But did that prove anything? Monk didn't know anybody—himself included—who believed in werewolves, vampires, zombies, or anything else of that ilk. IRS agents and blood-sucking Wall Street bankers were the only monsters he knew. And maybe a few lawyers and some Republicans. How could he believe Harold Lanack changed into a vicious animal when the moon is full? A wolf man that played golf?

On the one hand, it might be the big story that ensured Monk's job for years to come—with maybe a Pulitzer to boot. On the other, what if he was wrong? Forget the retirement package. They'd laugh him out of the union and the *Herald* would fire him for impersonating a reporter. Bye-bye pension.

Monk tried to get the idea out of his mind and get back to work. He had a formidable task at hand, making sense out of gibberish that Dan Stacey had filed about the Yankees signing Roger Clemens to come out of retirement and pitch them into the World Series. This time, Stacey had not only buried the lead but most of the salient facts—like whether Clemens was in jail or not at the time of the signing. Monk put down his silver pen and turned back to the computer screen.

He finished the rewrite with fifteen minutes to spare even though the Harold Lanack werewolf story made it almost impossible to concentrate. He knew he'd never get to sleep unless he settled the question one way or the other, so he dug through the pile of notes on his desk until he found the list of dates he'd compiled earlier. He stared at the piece of paper, doodled on the edges, rolled it up and beat on the desk with it, but he couldn't think of any way to prove his wild theory other than stalking Lanack during the next full moon.

When would that be? Monk flipped over his desk calendar and counted four weeks from the British Open. He came to the third weekend in August, the date of the PGA Championship at Winged Foot. The final major in the Grand Slam.

Sleep was now out of the question. Monk had to get to the truth about Harold Lanack. He unrolled the list of dates and started putting them in order on a fresh sheet. When he got to the Masters this year, he remembered the ugly killing of the feminist that Saturday night. As he jotted a note next to the dates, he recalled the tourist who died at the Tour Players Championship. Add the socialite killed at Shinnecock and Colin Montgomerie's weird death at Carnoustie, and a bloody pattern emerged. Inspired, Monk turned back to the computer and searched each of the dates and locations of Lanack's wins on tour outside the majors. By the time he finished, the newsroom was deserted, the sun was rising over New York, and Monk had linked a murder to every win.

Bleary eyed, Monk drove home convinced he had a hot story. As he fell into bed, though, another possibility arose. What if Lanack wasn't the moon-mad killer? Another person was in the same places on the exact same dates—Vlad Krajivek. Maybe the caddie was the werewolf. Maybe they both were! Monk's mind whirred faster and faster. Then he remembered one of Lanack's wins he hadn't checked out, the first one.

* * *

That night in the newsroom, Monk did his best to find the details surrounding Harold Lanack's victory in the Austrian Open. He figured out the phase of the moon for the tournament dates, and the full moon did indeed fall on Saturday night. Searching the online editions of *Der Kurier*, the only Viennese paper with an English language edition, he found a story about a suspicious death that fit the pattern too. He thought for a moment he had proved his case until he read further and discovered something utterly confounding: a woman had been charged and convicted of the murder. Her name was Maria Krajivek.

Monk got on the phone and finally, after much cajoling, blustering, and even a little wheedling with various Austrian bureaucrats, discovered that Maria Krajivek had been declared insane and was an involuntary inmate in *Psychiatrisches Krankenhaus Baumgartner Höhe*, a psychiatric hospital in Vienna. The not very informative administrator of the hospital told him there was no way he could speak to her by telephone. She was allowed visitors only during certain times and the window of opportunity would close in ten days. Monk glanced at his calendar and did some quick calculations.

"That would be during the full moon," he said. "Is there a reason for that?"

"Yes," the administrator answered. "Like many of our patients, Frau Krajivek becomes easily agitated when the moon is full."

Monk considered going to Charlie Stogel with his werewolf story and plea for travel funds for a trip to Austria to confirm it, but knew that would be like asking the Pope for money to put another coat of paint on the ceiling of the Sistine Chapel. But it was possible—not likely but possible—that he could get a budget to do an interview with Harold Lanack, which might give him a chance to somehow get confirmation face-to-face.

The next morning, he called Byron Levine, director of PGA media relations and an old buddy, and asked for help in arranging an interview with the hard-to-reach Lanack.

Levine snickered. "You're not going to ask any questions about the full moon, are you?" Before Monk could answer, he added, "I'll see what I can do."

Monk was shocked when the answer came within a few hours. Levine said he was surprised, too, but Lanack would give him an hour at his home in Orlando. Monk was nearly as shocked when Charlie Stogel signed off on it—as long as Monk could fly to Orlando, get the interview, and fly back the same day so the paper wouldn't have to spring for a hotel room. It helped that Sully was covering baseball between the golf majors in the perpetually short-staffed *Herald* sports department. Monk didn't care why. He set up the trip before anyone could change their minds.

Lanack wasn't alone when Monk got to his house. Vlad Krajivek was in the lanai, sucking down a Bloody Mary and scowling. Great, Monk thought, two werewolves for the price of one.

"So tell me," Monk began after he'd refused a Bloody Mary of his own. "How do you like your chances to win the Grand Slam?"

"They are good," Lanack said. That was it. His answer. No elaboration. Monk sensed it was going to be a long, difficult sixty minutes.

"What's your strategy for Winged Foot?" Monk tried again.

"Hit ball in fairway, stay below hole, sink putt."

Very insightful, Monk thought. The readers would hang on every word when he wrote this up. He tried to keep the sarcasm out of his next question.

"How much extra pressure do you feel?"

"None."

"You aren't worried about your opponents?" As soon as the words left his lips, Monk realized he'd committed sin number one: he'd asked a question that could be answered "yes" or "no," not that it mattered with this guy.

Sure enough, Lanack replied, "No."

That was enough for Monk. "Look, Harold, why did you agree to this interview?"

Lanack exchanged looks with Krajivek.

"Harold is an exceptional golfer, as I am sure you would agree." Krajivek said. Monk nodded. "The question you asked at Shinnecock demonstrated that you are exceptional in your field as well. Harold wanted his first in-depth interview to be with someone of your caliber."

Sirens went off in Monk's head as his bullshit detector flashed red, redder, reddest. But at least he had an opening to the full moon connection. Still, he wondered what they really wanted.

"That's very flattering," Monk said. "So do you want to answer the question now?"

"It is still stupid question," Lanack growled. When Krajivek glared at him, he tried to smile and added a just-kidding "Heh, heh, heh."

Krajivek interjected, "What Harold means is, why do you ask?"

Now Monk got it. They wanted to know how much he knew. That was good and bad. Good because it gave him a chance to possibly confirm the connection between the full moon murders and Harold Lanack. Bad because he was alone with two killers who would probably prefer that he not leave the room alive if he did.

Choosing his words very, very carefully, Monk said, "It was just a coincidence I happened to notice. As you know, we journalists are always fishing for a new angle." He couldn't resist a "Heh, heh, heh" of his own.

"I see," Krajivek said. Monk didn't think the caddie bought his line, but it gave Monk a little time.

"One more question, please," Monk said. "If the full moon isn't a factor, how do you explain your exemplary performances on Sundays? I mean, no offense, but that's the only day when you stand out from the pack." Monk wished he hadn't said "pack."

Krajivek answered before Lanack had a chance. "I often prepare a special meal for Harold when he is in contention. An old family recipe that brings him strength. It is a little superstition of ours, like your American football players eating spaghetti and fried chicken before a big game."

Monk had never heard of that one, but it wasn't relevant. "But only when he's in contention?"

Lanack answered, "Yes, otherwise the ritual would lose its significance, don't you see?"

"And what is this special meal?" Monk asked.

Krajivek answered this time. "Liver. Liver cooked very, very rare."

Lanack added, "Bloody. Heh, heh, heh,"

Monk didn't have any follow-up to that. He also didn't like the way Lanack's eyes lit up at the mention of bloody organs, so he made his excuses, stuck his pen back in his pocket, and headed for the airport while he still had his own liver.

Was Harold Lanack a moon-maddened killer? Monk had no doubt, but he also had no proof. He had to interview the only person who might have an answer, Maria Krajivek. If the *NY Herald* wouldn't spring for the trip, Monk decided, he'd dig into his own savings.

Monk wrote up his meager notes on the flight back to New York, filed the story as soon as he got to the newsroom, and went home to get some sleep.

When he got to work the next afternoon, he found a note from Charlie Stogel stuck to the center of his computer screen. "See Me NOW" it read in bright red letters. Monk went straight to Stogel's office, not sure what to expect.

When he opened the door, Stogel didn't say "hello." He said, "Liver!" Then he shouted just in case Monk missed the point. "Liver in the moonlight? I give you an expense-paid trip to Orlando and you give me liver?!" Stogel snapped open a copy of that morning's paper and thrust the interview with Harold Lanack in Monk's face.

"I, uh," Monk stammered.

"I swear, Monk, you really ought to retire—right away before you do something stupid like this again. I can't believe the best angle you could find on the biggest story in golf in the last century is what Harry the Closer eats for dinner. Jesus!"

"Now, Charlie, there's a lot more to this story," Monk explained. "But I need to confirm a couple of things before we break it. I guarantee you—it's big. Bigger than the Grand Slam."

"What?" Stogel snapped. "He eats oatmeal on Sunday morning to clean the rare liver from his colon?"

"No! Really! I just need a couple of days in Vienna to pull it together."

"Vienna? Vienna as in Austria?" Stogel's bushy eyebrows climbed his forehead. "You want me to send you to Vienna to write a story about the Grand Slam? Or is it about Harry Lanack's caddie's recipe for Linzer Torte? Get out of my office before I begin your retirement today!"

Monk ducked out the door as the newspaper flew at his head.

The next day, he put in for a vacation, which Stogel immediately approved. The air fare to Vienna made a major dent in Monk's savings, but what the heck, he didn't really need a membership in the Dunes when he retired. There are plenty of very reasonable and perfectly good daily fee courses in Myrtle Beach and maybe he could get a part time job as a ranger at one of them when Charlie Stogel fired him. In the meantime, he had to get the real story on Harold Lanack.

* * *

When he arrived at the *Psychiatrisches Krankenhaus Baumgartner Höhe*, Monk found the hospital administrator much more helpful in person than he had been on the telephone.

"Frau Krajivek is Roma," the doctor explained, "so many of her delusions are tied into gypsy fables and fairy stories. As you will see, she says the murder was part of a strange ritual staged by her husband. However, the evidence against her was conclusive."

"What was the evidence?" Monk asked.

"She was found near the crime scene covered in the victim's blood. She was in a deranged state and babbling incoherently, but her fingerprints were found on the murder weapon, a silver dinner knife that belonged to her."

Monk thought the evidence sounded a little circumstantial, but he kept his opinion to himself.

"Who was the victim?"

"An unfortunate man, a groundskeeper who lived on the golf course where the murder occurred. His wife said he had gone out into the night to chase off a pack of stray dogs they heard howling on the course. The dogs were never found. The police believe the howls came from Frau Krajivek in her disturbed state."

"Who found her?"

"Her husband. He and a friend, a professional golfer I believe, became worried when they came home after a late dinner and didn't find her in the house."

Now Monk was sure the woman was framed.

"Can I see her now?" he asked.

"Yes, but I must ask you to leave all sharp objects with my secretary, please." The doctor pointed to the silver pen in Monk's hand.

The *Psychiatrisches Krankenhaus Baumgartner Höhe* didn't resemble a grey-walled prison, but Monk supposed it operated like one. The flower-lined paths on the grounds went nowhere near the tasteful but tall wrought-iron perimeter fence, he noticed, and the hallways inside all led to wood-paneled doors that locked securely. He met Maria Krajivek in a homey day room furnished in chintz-covered chairs and comfy sofas and lit by sun-filled windows of wire-reinforced glass.

"My husband is evil," Maria said as soon as she sat down. She pulled a stray lock of gray hair back behind her ear as if to keep it from obstructing her view of Monk. There was no wildness in her dark eyes. They were wary.

"Tell me what happened," Monk said.

"I followed my husband when he went out that night. I thought he was seeing another woman but it turned out to be much worse. He met another man."

"Really? He was having an affair with a man?" Monk asked.

"No! I don't mean it in that way. He met the man he worked for at the golf tournament, and they went into the woods on the course. I hid behind a tree and listened as my husband—an evil, evil man—told the golfer he could make him invincible."

"What did the golfer do?"

"He nodded," Maria said. "As if they had discussed it before. Then my husband whistled and the hounds of hell came to him."

"The what?" Monk said. He didn't like the way her dark eyes kept getting wider and wider, but he desperately wanted to hear the end of the story before they came and threw a net over her again.

"The hounds of hell! The wolves that aren't wolves. The men who aren't men."

"Oh," Mark said.

"My husband made a sign and the wolves surrounded them. The golfer tried to run away, but the leader of the pack knocked him to the ground and sank his fangs into his throat. My husband howled and howled and the others joined in with him."

Monk felt the hair on the back of his neck stand up.

"That is when the other man—the groundskeeper—came out of the trees. He must have been hiding like me, but the wolves saw him and ran him to the ground. As my husband jumped into the middle of the pack, something gleamed in the moonlight. My husband stabbed and stabbed the poor man while the wolves howled and danced."

Monk swallowed, hard. "What about the golfer?"

"As the other man fell, he arose. He had become a wolf on two legs. He lifted his snout and bayed at the moon rising over the tree tops."

"I don't understand," Monk said. "I thought he was dead."

"He was, but the bite of the werewolf transformed him. Only a silver weapon can kill a werewolf—you should know that. Once a man is bitten by the wolf, he will turn unless he is killed again. Immediately. Death must come by a silver bullet or a knife like my husband used on the groundskeeper."

"Then what happened?"

"I do not know. I swooned. When I awoke my dress was soaked in the dead man's blood. I screamed, but the only ones there to hear me were my husband and the golfer. They held me until the police came."

"And the police did not believe your story?" Monk asked.

The woman looked around at the wire-meshed windows, the locked door, the attendant watching her every move from across the room. "What do you think?" she said.

Sheepishly, Monk nodded. "Your husband and the golfer are free," he said. "What can be done about them?"

The woman stared into his face. Monk looked back steadily, trying to show he was sincere. Finally, she said, "You must seek out Timea the fortune teller in the village of Mayrhof. She will tell you what to do."

* * *

Timea proved easy to find in the decrepit village of Mayrhof. Her house was the one with the sign in the window that said "Fortune Teller." Monk knocked, and sure enough, he was greeted by a wart-nosed crone wearing gold earrings and draped with multi-colored shawls. When he told her who sent him and what he wanted to know, she led him into a dark parlor lit by a single lamp set on a small cloth-covered table between two wooden chairs in the center of the room. The walls were hung with star charts and mystic drawings of long-gowned maidens, unicorns, and hairy-chested satyrs.

Timea sat down and motioned for Monk to join her.

"Are you strong of heart?" she said.

"Uh, I guess so," Monk replied.

"You must be strong of heart to prevail in your quest. Let me see the palm of your hand."

Monk laid his hand on the table. The old woman leaned over it, mumbling under her breath as she spread his fingers and turned the palm back and forth in the dim light. After maybe two minutes of muttering and clucking to herself, she straightened up in her chair, looked him in the eye, and said "You can kill the lycanthrope."

Monk wasn't sure whether he should feel relieved or on guard, so he just said, "How?"

"The deed must be done by the light of the moon and the fatal wound must be inflicted by a silver weapon."

"Like in the movies? A silver bullet?" Monk asked.

"Yes. Like in the movies," she sighed. "Do you have a gun?"

"I've got a 38 police special I got when I was covering a mob trial years ago," Monk said. "I don't know if it even works."

"You had best find out. Do you have a silver bullet?"

"Uh, no."

"For a small price, I will give you the bullet you need."

There goes the rest of my savings, Monk thought. As he reached for his wallet, he thought of something else. "There are two of them, I think. I'm not sure which one is the werewolf."

"Then you must kill them both," the old woman said. "You will need two silver bullets."

"I was afraid you were going to say that."

The old woman disappeared through a curtain in the back of the room and came back with a small leather pouch. As she laid it in Monk's hand, she said, "Aim true and be of strong heart."

* * *

Monk got back to New York the weekend before the PGA Championship, the fourth and final tournament in the Grand Slam. The city was crazy for Harry the Closer. His exploits ran in endless loops on all the TV outlets, not just the Golf Channel, alternating with grainy black and white film of Bobby Jones' triumphal ticker tape parade in 1930. Nike, one of Lanack's new-found sponsors, put up a four-story digital billboard in Times Square that ran images of their latest champion lofting each of the three major trophies he'd won so far this year. Talk radio was jammed with amazingly ignorant callers telling the world Harold Lanack was a.) the greatest athlete since Achilles, b.) working on a cure for cancer in his spare time, or c.) the antichrist and, since he was European, probably a Socialist to boot. Monk found it all amazing and more than a little scary. It was also confusing. He knew what he had to do, but he couldn't figure out how to do it.

Winged Foot was even more convenient for Monk than Shinnecock had been. Not only was it less than an hour's drive from Manhattan, it was only about ten minutes from his house in Pelham. He went to the course Tuesday to look for opportunities. Standing far back at the practice range for the pros that had been built on the East Course, he saw Lanack surrounded by guards hired to keep the crowds at bay and to protect him from a maniac with a pistol in their pocket and deadly intentions on their mind—just like Monk. With his press pass he could get close enough to put the silver bullet in Lanack's heart, but he probably wouldn't survive to collect his Pulitzer.

Wednesday, Monk followed Lanack around the course during his practice round, trying to stay well back in the crowd that swarmed behind the ropes. At the walkway near the seventh green, though, the crowd surged and pushed him forward just as Lanack walked by to go to the next tee. He didn't stop, but he gave Monk a cold-eyed grin as he strutted by. On the eighth tee, he whispered something to Krajivek, then nodded in Monk's direction. After Lanack hit his drive, the caddie said something to one of the guards, but Monk slipped away into the crowd.

That night in the newsroom, Monk had trouble concentrating on the job at hand, which was editing the numerous reports on the tournament, the course, the players, and the most distracting of all, the miles of copy about Harold Lanack's pursuit of the Grand Slam. Dan Stacey's story about Rory McIlroy and the other top challengers had to be translated from cliché-ridden nonsense to intelligible reporting, Sully's worshipful profile of Harold Lanack had to be toned to down to simple adulation, and his own piece on the challenges of Winged Foot had to be cut to fit the news hole.

Monk read through what he'd written about the bloody 1974 U.S. Open, known as the "Massacre at Winged Foot" and decided that had to stay. He cut the paragraph about Billy Casper's lay-up strategy on the second hole in the 1959 Open because it would be of interest mostly to a small number of golf aficionados, as well as the one about Fuzzy Zoeller's towel-waving antics in 1984, mainly because he didn't much like Fuzzy. For obvious reasons, he left in the brief account of Bobby Jones' 1929 U.S. Open victory, and, mostly out of sentimentality, he kept the description of Davis Love's 1997 PGA Championship win even though pictures of the timely rainbow that appeared over the eighteenth green always left Monk vaguely nauseated. His story ended by telling how Phil Mickelson blew his chance to win the U.S. Open in 2006. He added a short note that Colin Montgomerie, who threw away his own shot at the title on the same hole a few minutes before Phil, had been killed four weeks ago.

As he was finishing his piece, Sully strolled up to his desk. With a smirk, he said, "You were in demand at the course today."

"By who?"

"You mean 'by whom.' As an editor you should know that. It was Vlad Krajivek. He grabbed me and asked if you were going to be at Lanack's press conference after the practice round. I told him I didn't know, which I didn't. Where were you, by the way? I didn't think you'd miss another chance to follow up on the full moon raw liver conspiracy."

"Very funny!" Monk said.

Sully left laughing.

* * *

Grand Slam mania abated a bit once the tournament got underway Thursday and everyone realized Harold Lanack couldn't win on the first day. He had to play four rounds of grueling, punishing golf while holding off the challenges from 155 other golfers who wanted to win, too.

Lanack played accordingly. He didn't take any chances, he didn't make any mistakes, and he ended up well behind the first-day leaders. In his comment after the round, he was icy calm. "I am content with my performance today," he said. "There is much golf to be played."

And much blood to be spilled, Monk thought as he put the next morning's edition to bed and left for the night. He waved to the night watchman and exited the *NY Herald* building onto 42nd Street, the same short route he walked every night to the garage two blocks away. Monk hadn't quite reached the corner when he caught a stealthy movement out of the corner of his eye. He wasn't sure, but he thought he saw someone slip into a dark doorway in the block ahead, a dark doorway he passed every night to get to the garage. Uncertain, he slowed to time his walk so he had to wait for the light to cross Third Avenue.

As he watched the doorway in the block ahead, a knot of noisy revelers spilled out of a bar on the other side of Third and turned the corner onto 42nd Street. Monk dashed across the street against the light, ignoring the angry blast of a taxi that barely missed him. On the other side, Monk slipped to the curb and matched his pace to the gang of partiers, keeping them between himself and the doorway as they walked by.

A rumpled figure slumped head down in the shadows of the doorway, but Monk couldn't tell if it was a bum taking a leak or Harold Lanack ready to cut his heart out. He didn't hang around to find out.

* * *

Just as he had done on Thursday, Monk stayed away from Lanack at Winged Foot on Friday. The fortune teller may have seen a strong heart when she examined his palm, but Monk was having his doubts.

Lanack's play was again unspectacular, but he easily made the cut and stood six shots behind the leaders going into Saturday's round. As Monk was editing the day's wrap up, Sully came in.

"Your buddy was looking for you again today," he said.

"My buddy?"

"Yeah. Krajivek. He grabbed me in the parking lot. Said something weird."

"He's a weird guy," Monk said, trying to sound nonchalant. "What did he say?"

"He asked me why you weren't at the tournament. Wanted to know if you were afraid of something."

"Of what?"

"How the hell do I know?" Sully scoffed. "Then he asked me if you lived in Pelham. Said he found an E. Monk in the phonebook and thought it might be you."

Monk sat up so fast his chair scooted backwards. "What did you tell him?"

"I said 'yeah.' Why? What's going on?"

"Nothing," Monk said. "I, uh, just don't want the guy, you know, sending me flowers or anything."

"You know something, Monk?" Sully said with a chuckle that broadened into a laugh, "You're as weird as he is."

When Monk left that night, he used the side entrance to the building and walked all the way to 40th Street before circling around to come into the garage from the other direction. He didn't want to tempt any dark figures was waiting for him the shadows.

All the way home, he thought about Krajivek asking where he lived. By the time he got to the parkway, he wished he had brought his gun with the silver bullets instead of leaving it in the nightstand next to his bed.

Monk usually got home around three in the morning when all of his neighbors were fast asleep and his street was stone dead quiet. Almost everyone put their cars in their garages or driveways overnight, although a few either had one too many cars or so much junk in their garage they parked at the curb. As Monk drove down the street, every parked car seemed out of place and just a touch unfamiliar. The shadows cast by the nearly full moon made their interiors dark and menacing.

As Monk slowed to turn into his driveway, he spotted a car parked across the street from his house that definitely didn't belong on his working-class block. It was much too new and upscale. As he pulled even with it, he saw it was a Mercedes—just like the courtesy cars provided to the players at the tournament. Monk didn't bother looking inside. He stomped on the gas and sped away. As he made a too-fast turn at the end of the block, he saw the Mercedes backing into his driveway to turn around.

Monk had to get somewhere safe, some place with people. He zigged and zagged through the neighborhood streets until he got to Post Road, then sped east to the New Rochelle diner. Even at three in the morning, he knew the 24-hour eatery would have a small crowd. Not many of them sober, but potential witnesses none the less. He parked in the back out of sight from the street and spent the rest of the night nursing black coffee and keeping one eye on the traffic while he tried to figure out how he was going to kill Harold Lanack later that night.

By the time the lunch crowd started to filter in, Monk decided it would be safe to go home. Lanack would be at the course by now getting ready to tee off for the third round. Monk's eyes were grainy and his stomach sour from way too much coffee and angst. He wanted a shower, maybe even a nap. He also had to get the pistol with its silver bullets. After about the fifth cup of coffee, he had decided that the only way to stop Harold Lanack was to follow him from Winged Foot after the day's round and ambush him wherever he was staying. It was risky, but it was the only plan his sleep-deprived brain could devise.

It turned out not to be necessary. When Monk walked in the front door, his answering machine was blinking. He pushed the button and recognized the voice right away. It was Vlad Krajivek.

"If you want an exclusive interview with Harold Lanack on the eve of the greatest triumph in golf, meet me at midnight at the west entrance to the locker room."

The appeal to his vanity as a reporter was crude, Monk thought, but much more effective than an ambush on 42nd Street. It also neatly solved Lanack's need for a victim the night before the final round while eliminating the one person who suspected him of being more than a really, really good golfer. Meeting at midnight was kind of heavy-handed and a bit overly dramatic, Monk thought, but the location was ideal—a dark passageway between the clubhouse and the pro shop not far from the tenth tee. A perfect spot for a murder.

The decision made, Monk showered, shaved, and loaded his 38 police special with the two silver bullets. Then he settled into his easy chair to watch the third round of the championship on TV. He needed to rest—and to strengthen his heart—for tonight.

Monk paid barely any attention to the results of the third round. Lanack ended the day tied for the lead with Dustin Johnson, who had a record of collapsing in the final round of the majors. There were a half dozen players within three strokes of the leaders, but Harold Lanack had a lock on the trophy—and the Grand Slam—unless Monk changed the path of destiny.

Before he left, Monk checked the pistol again and tucked it into this belt, where it was pointed directly at his testicles. Not good. He tried in both front and back pants pockets, but couldn't get it out easily enough. Finally, he put on his jacket and stuck the pistol in the inner breast pocket next to his lucky pen. Perfect.

Monk drove to the Fenimore Road entrance at Winged Foot ready to flash his credentials and give the guard what he hoped was a valid-sounding story about needing to retrieve his laptop from the press tent. He didn't need the story. The tall iron gates were open and the guard lay in a bloody heap near one of the stone pillars.

Monk almost turned around on the spot. I'm not cut out for this, he thought. What good will a Pulitzer Prize do me if I'm dead? Besides, I'm supposed to retire. Hell, now I want to retire! But he fought off the panic. After a few minutes of deep breathing, he got out and left his car near the gate. No way was he going to just drive into an ambush. He had another idea.

He walked as quietly as he could through the trees on the left, working his way around to the yard of the house behind the tenth green, the one with the bedroom window Ben Hogan said he aimed at when he played the hole. He climbed the fence, skirted the TV tower behind the green, and made his way behind the grandstands on his right so he could stay in the shadows of the trees screening the parking lot. His knees got weaker with every step, but he pressed forward. Taking a deep breath, he stepped out onto the tenth tee and into the brilliant light of the full moon.

He was just a few steps from the passageway between the pro shop and the locker room entrance but he couldn't see anyone in the shadows. They were probably in the doorway waiting to jump him, he thought. Summoning what little courage he had left, Monk was about to call out to Lanack when Vlad Krajivek stepped out of the passage.

The caddie walked slowly toward Monk, a feral grin on his face, his hands held out to show they were empty. Monk fumbled in his jacket and pulled out the gun anyway.

"That's close enough," Monk said. "Where's Lanack?"

Krajivek stopped at the edge of the tee box, five paces from Monk. "He'll join us soon," he said. Then he took another cautious step.

"I said stop!" Monk said. He waved the gun vaguely in Krajivek's direction.

The caddie stopped, his grin widened for a moment, then he puckered his lips and gave a low whistle.

Harold Lanack—or what was once Harold Lanack—emerged from the shadows into the moonlight. The werewolf was a least a head taller than the golfer whose soul he had captured. His broad hairy chest tapered to lanky hips and long, muscular legs. Claws like daggers gleamed in the moonlight. The creature may have stood upright on two legs, but it wasn't human. Its face wasn't Harry the Closer's either, nor any other man's. Pointed ears stuck out from tangled hair. Yellow eyes glowered under heavy brows. A long, thin muzzle jutted from between the eyes, the black snout sniffing its prey while a string of spittle ran from the sharp teeth below.

Transfixed, Monk almost missed the lunge Krajivek made. The caddie was a step away when Monk pulled the trigger. Krajivek's chest exploded in a cloud of red mist. At the sound of the shot, Lanack let loose a howl so long and loud it must have shattered windows.

The howl certainly shattered what was left of Monk's strong heart. He turned and ran down the fairway, desperate to reach the fence beyond the green 190 yards away.

The creature howled again, then sprinted after Monk. His claws tore up the turf as he bounded across the grass on all fours. Monk was nearly at the green before he remembered the gun. He turned, extended his shaking arm, and fired at the werewolf charging toward him. The shot rang out, but the creature didn't even slow. Monk had missed with his last silver bullet.

Panicked, he turned to run across the green. Silver! Monk had to have a silver weapon. Just as Monk got to the pin, which was cut in the front of the green for Sunday's final round, the monster leapt. Monks' foot caught the flag stick and he fell, the werewolf's outstretched claws just missing his face. Monk tumbled over the edge of the deep bunker beside the green. As he rolled to the bottom, his jacket twisted around him and his silver pen jabbed his chest. He pulled it out and thrust it upward with all his desperate strength as Lanack dived off the green onto him.

* * *

Monk went home from the hospital after only a couple of days of observation. The district attorney said he would need to testify before the grand jury, but that was mostly a formality since all the evidence pointed to self-defense. Two rent-a-cops said they heard the gun shots and the howls and saw Lanack attacking him on the tenth green. They also found blood, hair, and bits of uniform from the dead guard on Fenimore Road stuck to Krajivek. The only mystery that remained, as far as the district attorney was concerned, was why Lanack was naked.

Back at the newsroom, Monk wrote the inside story of the wolf man who almost won the Grand Slam. The Pulitzer was a lock so Charlie Stogel took retirement off the table but Monk didn't really care anymore. The only thing on his mind was the bite healing much too slowly under the massive bandage on his neck. Somehow, he was sure it would itch like mad the next time the moon was full.

A Rant And Ramble

Into The Origins Of Golf

Who invented golf? Common wisdom says it was the Scots, but that's poppycock. Golf has been around much longer than they have. The evidence, like the fossil record that verifies evolution, is all around. You just have to know what to look for. If you dig into it as I have, you'll be surprised at what you find.

But let me deal with the Scots first. I am one, at least fractionally, so I can say what I darn well please about the tribe. The first documented evidence of golf in Scotland appears in an Act of the Scottish Parliament in 1457, in which King James II prohibited the game because it was distracting his soldiers from archery practice. Either the Scots couldn't read or they just didn't give a damn, because the game was outlawed again in 1471 and once more in 1491. Finally, King James the whatever gave up and just let them play.

One reason the Scots lay claim to having invented golf is that they created the eighteen hole course. This wasn't one of their brighter ideas. Until they codified it, a golf course could have as many holes as you wanted, although multiples of three seemed to be most popular. Nine is actually a much better number of holes for a round. Nine holes you can play in about the same amount of time it takes to play a tennis match.

Eighteen holes, though, take half a day that turns into a full day by the time you add the obligatory recovery stop at the nineteenth hole for liquid refreshments and settlement of wagers. Nine holes you can squeeze in before work and blame your tardiness on traffic. Eighteen holes requires a day out of the office excused by a whopper like your brother-in-law got arrested in Tijuana and you had to go bail him out—again.

The Scots may not have invented golf, but they can be credited—or blamed—for several other flaws in the game in addition to making it take all day. For example, it was their brilliant idea to make the hole too damned small. They could have made it any size at all—I'm thinking as big around as a bucket would be good. That would give a guy a decent chance to get up and down for an occasional par. But no, the Scots decreed the cup had to be a miniscule four inches in diameter, the perfect size for only one thing: generating lip outs.

And pot bunkers! The Scots made their bunkers so small you need to take your shoes off just so both feet fit in the litter box. And how are you supposed to swing a club in there? It's like trying to pitch out of a telephone booth. Legend has it that bunkers were originally hollows in the ground made by sheep hunkering down to get out of the wind and rain. Fine. Let the sheep have the pot bunkers. Build us some real ones.

Then there is the single worst invention in the history of golf, bagpipes. You can blame those over-engineered whoopee cushions on the Scots, too. What's really sad is that the Scots think what comes out of them is music.

As I mentioned before I got distracted, there is much evidence that golf predates the Scots. They may have messed up the game, but they didn't invent it. There's just too much evidence to the contrary.

Just look at the rack, that medieval torture device you see in all the cartoons. It could just as easily be a golf training aid later adopted to the modern game by Jim McLean. Where do you think he got the "X Factor"? And speaking of golf lessons, check out those Egyptian drawings where everybody walks around with their feet on sideways and their elbows screwed on backwards. Did you ever see anything that more closely resembles a golf instruction book? Or Sumerian cuneiform, which emerged around 3000 BC? Looks exactly like a scorecard using the Stableford system. There is a lot of evidence if you just know where to look.

Traces of ancient golf courses are everywhere. Those massive Nazca lines you can only see from the air over Peru are obviously remnants of a ridiculously long par five. The great pyramids of Egypt? Moguls left from a prototype Pete Dye par four. Heck, the man is old enough to have built them himself. And the original island green par three? The Galapagos, of course, before it was overrun by tortoises and blue footed boobies. Or it might even have been Mount Ararat, which Noah could barely reach with a five iron from the deck of the Ark.

Speaking of islands, the stone heads of Easter Island look exactly like the portraits of bankers, lawyers, industrialists, and robber barons lining the halls of many country clubs today. Could their forbearers have run an exclusive club in the middle of the Pacific?

I'm jumping around the time line a bit, but the first cart girl may well have been Marie Antoinette, who said, "Let them eat cake" after a bunch of testosterone-addled drunks on the front nine gave her so much crap she refused to go out after they made the turn. And mini golf was certainly not invented in New Jersey. It was actually created in pre-historic England. You can see the remains of the course at Stonehenge.

The ancient Mayans played golf, too. And being the mathematical geniuses they were, they invented the forerunner of today's handicap system, complete with course ratings, slope, and the ever-popular handicap index that's often depicted on round stone carvings. Equitable Stroke Control came later, though, and possibly caused the downfall of the civilization.

No, if you want to find the origins of golf, you have to go far, far back in time to the Garden of Eden, also known as the Mesopotamian National Golf Resort and Spa. It says in Genesis that God took Adam's rib and created Eve, but that's a stretch. Logic tells you it's impossible to create an entire woman out of a hunk of bone. A golf club, now that's an entirely do-able feat of engineering.

Golf balls weren't any big problem, either. There was a nice big tree full of spherical fruit that worked just fine. Which brings us to the moral of the story, which further proves my point.

Everything was beautiful there in the Garden. Adam played golf nearly every day. It was a time of innocence and wonder, so his drives were straight and true, his short game accurate and deadly. Eve didn't play, but she was happy for Adam and spent most of her time puttering around in the Garden and taking yoga classes.

Classes taught by whom, you ask? By the snake, of course, and therein lies one of the great tragedies of history. It was the snake who whispered in Eve's ear. "It's a shame Adam spends so much time on the golf course," he hissed. "Don't you wish he cared as much about you as he does his precious Big Bertha?"

You know the rest of the story. Eve, not wanting to go down in history as the first golf widow, put on a snit. When Adam came home from the course—late, naturally—she snatched the apple out of his bag and took a big bite out of it. As Adam tried to sputter a protest, she thrust the half-eaten fruit into his face and demanded he prove his love for her by eating the rest of it.

"But honey, you know you're the most important thing in my life," Adam pleaded. "Besides, I just picked that ball this morning. It's a brand new Pro V!"

"Eat it!" she screeched. "Or you can just go sleep in the locker room at your precious golf club!"

Adam knew he was beat. He took the apple from her hand, silently mourned its ruined perfection, and swallowed it whole. The schmuck.

God found out the next day on the first tee when Adam teed up a rock.

"What happened to that Pro V I created for you?" He asked.

"I, uh, lost it," Adam stammered. He was a lousy liar.

Suspicious, God asked, "How? You had it when we walked off the eighteenth yesterday. Did you play another round without me?"

Adam didn't know what to say. It never did any good to lie to God, so he told Him the whole sordid story.

God became royally peeved.

"Get out!" he thundered. "From this day forward you will wander the earth and play only daily fee municipal courses—on weekends when your wife allows! What's more, on the rare occasions when you do play, you will be afflicted by a swing that shall forever remind you of that evil snake. Your ball will twist and curve in the air. From now on, you will slice."

And thus did golf as we know it come to be.

By The Rules

Sully had a hog-splitting headache. Not a little tension in the neck or a dull thump around the temples. Not some uncomfortable tightness across the scalp or pressure behind the eyeballs. No, Sully had a thunderbolt-from-Olympus-someone-drove-over-my-head-with-a-tractor-please-kill-me-so-I'll-feel-better headache.

As best he could remember last night—which wasn't very well—he had foolishly taken on Tom Marigold at shots. Silly game, shots. Also deadly. Each man threw three darts for a total score, and the loser bought a shot and a beer. The winner got the beer, which he could drink at his leisure, while the loser took the shot, which he had to down immediately. If you got off to a bad start, as Sully did last night, the shots came quick and your aim deteriorated exponentially. The game could have very ugly consequences, some unforeseen and indirect, like today's.

"You've got Mr. Misky and Mr. Jay," Jimmy the caddie master said. The pain in Sully's head went up a notch.

"Great," he said. "The jerk brigade."

"Sorry, Sully, that's what happens when you get here last. Get their bags out, would you?"

Sure, Sully thought, I'll get their bags out. I'll haul their bags, I'll listen to them gripe at me all day, and then I'll take their big whopping tip over to the snack stand and buy a Coke—a small one. Sully briefly considered just disappearing, but he couldn't afford to get on the caddie master's bad side, especially since he couldn't remember how much money he lost to Marigold last night. He lugged the bags out to the rack.

"Hey Jimmy," he said, "I thought you were going to tell Misky to get a bag that doesn't take two men and a large boy to carry?"

"I did. He said I needed to hire stronger caddies. Fewer 'wimps and wussies,' if I remember right."

"Great, thanks for the help," Sully said as he went back into the bag room to get a towel and a caddie's smock. When he came back out into the glaring sun, the two golfers were standing by their bags.

"You gentlemen sure lucked out today," Jimmy fawned as Sully hefted Misky's bag onto one shoulder and reached for Jay's. "We're closing the course to get ready for the tournament right after you tee off, so you won't have anybody behind you. The group ahead of you teed off about a half hour ago."

"Is there only one caddie?" Misky asked. He looked at Sully with the same expression he might have worn when examining a cockroach on the sole of his shoe.

"Yes, sir," Jimmy answered.

"If that's the best you can do. . ." Misky said. He walked away toward the first tee.

"That's what we get for playing late," Jay pointed out as he followed behind. "You'll learn that after you've been a member for a few more years."

Misky was a new member this year and assumed he owned the club now that he had survived a six-year stint on the waiting list and had written a very large check for the privilege of playing with the old-money original members. His net worth was about the same size as his ego, which meant he could probably buy Delaware or Rhode Island should he want to. Neither his assets or his ego could buy him a legitimate single-digit handicap, however. In fact, if he didn't stretch the rules of golf far past the breaking point, his handicap would be closer to twenty than to the six he claimed.

Jay, on the other hand, was who Misky wanted to be—as long as he could keep his own bank account and subtract twenty years from Jay's age. Jay was a legacy member whose money was so old the bank notes were reportedly signed by Alexander Hamilton—by hand. Jay was also one of the club's better players, owing, no doubt, to the fact that he played six days a week and practiced on the seventh, something only people who clipped bond coupons for a living could do effectively. Jay loved the country club, lived for golf, and played strictly by the rules.

The finer distinctions between old money and new money were lost on Sully, of course, as was the sacred nature of the rules of golf. All he knew about his golfers was that they both considered a caddie an inferior species, located on the evolutionary ladder somewhere between a donkey and video store clerk. Jay was the slightly more considerate of the duo, but still made sure his caddie knew his place in the grand scheme of Western civilization.

Sully knew his place very well, so he shouldered the bags and trudged behind the men to the first tee.

The first hole is a middling par four with a generous fairway. The trouble on the course came later. The only danger off the first tee is on the left side, where the driving range is hidden behind a screen of trees and a line of out-of-bound stakes well away from the fairway. It took a snap hook with wings to get there, which is exactly what Misky hit. Sully watched the ball bounce once near the tree line, then disappear out of bounds. He mentally marked a locust tree with a split trunk where the ball was last seen.

"Looks like you're OB, Misky," Jay chortled.

"Nonsense," he answered. "It stayed in, didn't it, Sully?"

"Can't say for sure, Mr. Misky," Sully mumbled.

"You're a lot of help," Misky replied. "The hell with it, I'm taking a mulligan anyway."

Jay cleared his throat.

"You can hit a provisional, Misky," he said, "but no mulligans." The old man stared at him imperiously. Misky glared back for a moment.

"Fine, call it a provisional," he said between gritted teeth. He stepped up and hit a weak fade into the right rough thirty yards short of where Jay's ball lay in the middle of the fairway. "That's just great," he said as she stomped off the tee toward the trees to look for this first ball. Jay chuckled and followed him. Sully groaned as he settled the two big bags on his shoulders. The pain in his head flashed off and on like a neon bar sign. It is going to be a long day, he thought.

By the time Sully caught up with the two men, they were roaming in circles in the trees and out into the driving range yards away from where Misky's ball had landed. There were dozens of range balls scattered on both sides of the white OB stakes. Misky was busy on the in-bounds side lifting and checking balls so he could improve his lie if he happened to stumble on his ball, while Jay stayed out of bounds, happily convinced that his playing partner's ball was there. Sully walked straight to the tree and followed the line past it until he found Misky's ball nestled among the range balls eighteen inches past a white stake.

"Got it!" he called, the yell making his head ring. He picked up the ball and held it in the air for the two men to see before he slipped it into his smock and headed toward the fairway.

"Hey you! Caddie!" Misky shouted. "What do you think you're doing? That ball was fair! I saw it!" Sully froze in his track and a dark curtain of hurt flapped closed behind his eyes. This is not good, he thought.

"Uh, sorry, Mr. Misky," he said as the man huffed up red-faced and furious. "I swear it was out."

"You idiot! Don't you know better than to pick up a player's ball?" Misky raged. "What kind of caddie are you?"

"It was out," Jay said as he walked up. "I saw it, too." He couldn't have seen it until Sully held it up, of course, but he wasn't going to let Misky get away with anything.

"You're not going to defend this moron are you?" Misky asked incredulously.

"The caddie has nothing to do with it," Jay said. "I saw the ball and it was out of bounds." Misky glared at him for a second, then stomped off across the fairway.

When Misky got out of earshot, Jay said quietly, "It was OB, wasn't it, Sully?"

"Yes, sir, Mr. Jay."

"Good."

Sully was confused. Why would two men who obviously detested each other want to play golf? Four hours of snark and tension lay ahead, Sully knew. The thought didn't help his headache.

* * *

The late-morning July sun roasted the golf course as well as Sully's whiskey-dehydrated brain. He drank gallons of water but it seeped out of his pores as fast as he could gulp it down. His shirt was sweat-soaked and the bag straps chaffed on his shoulders. The two golfers seemed to play opposite sides of the fairway on every hole, so Sully had to trudge back and forth from one to the other, lugging the two bags and trying to ignore the red haze flickering off and on in the back of his eyeballs. He began to envy his brother, who had a nice, cushy job shoveling slag in a steel mill. It would be cooler there.

"Give me the driver," Misky snapped, jolting Sully out of his trance. The man's ball was on the cart path on the eleventh hole.

"No closer to the hole, Misky," Jay said pleasantly as he hovered nearby watching Misky measure the drop zone with his driver. The two men had quibbled over something on practically every hole. On the fourth, Sully thought Misky was going to bury his sand wedge in Jay's head when Jay caught him grounding his club in a bunker.

Now, Misky stood with his arm outstretched, trying to find a good lie. "Why don't you get off my back," Misky snarled. He dropped his ball and watched it bounce into a divot. He bent over and reached for it.

"It's a penalty if you touch that ball, Misky," Jay said.

"That was an accident, damn it! I didn't mean to drop there!"

"Sorry, you only get one drop under these circumstances. That's the rule."

"You! Caddie!" Misky jabbed his finger at Sully. "Is that right?" Sully was leaning heavily on Jay's bag. A bead of sweat dangled on the end of his nose and dripped off when he lifted his head to look blearily at Misky.

"Uh, yes sir. I guess so," he said. That was not the answer Misky wanted to hear, but Sully didn't have the strength to think of anything else but the truth.

"Screw you both," Misky growled. He kicked his ball out of the divot and into the fairway. He yanked an iron out of the bag and stamped away. Sully hoisted the bags and followed after him. He heard Jay mutter something like "that's about enough of that" behind his back.

Misky slashed viciously at his ball, sending it spinning in a long, high arc toward a creek that ran through the right side of the rough. The ball passed over the creek and plopped into the marshy grass on the other side. He roared and slung his club after it, then strode off, steaming, in the same direction. Sully walked over to Jay and watched him play his shot to the left side of the green two hundred yards away. He would have a long, long birdie putt. Then he followed as Jay headed toward Misky where he stood fuming on the creek bank. Sully hoped Jay would warn Misky about the area where his ball had landed. He didn't want to be the messenger delivering the bad news again.

The news would indeed be bad. Sully could see Misky's ball sitting up prettily on a tuft of grass in the marshy area on the other side of the creek. All Misky had to do was step over the narrow creek and he would have about a full wedge to the green. Of course, no member ever did that since the entire area was marked as a lateral hazard because that side of the creek was known to have deep pockets of quicksand scattered throughout.

"It's customary to take a penalty and drop on this side of the creek," Jay offered as Sully trudged up to the two men.

"I know the rules, you old fool," Misky hissed. "Give me my pitching wedge." Jay said nothing and gave Sully a long, cool look that gave him the shivers. Sully's much-abused head throbbed but he spoke up anyway as he pulled the club from the bag.

"I don't think. . ." Sully started to say.

"That's right. Don't think." Misky cut him off and yanked the club out of his hand. Misky leapt over the little creek and Jay held up his hand as Sully opened his mouth to protest.

"Be quiet, Sully," he said severely. "You know the player's the boss." Sully snapped his mouth shut.

Misky squished over the soft ground toward the ball. He cursed as one of his shoes almost got sucked off his foot but he finally took his stance and addressed the ball. "The rules cut both ways, Jay," he sneered. "No penalty if I play the ball out of the hazard." He lifted his head to check the distance to the green. He didn't notice the ooze rising silently up the sides of his shoes.

"Just remember," Jay called cheerfully, "you can't ground your club." Misky glanced down involuntarily just in time to snatch the sole of his wedge from the grass behind the ball. At the same time, the mud rose over his shoe tops. He realized he was now a couple of inches closer to the ball, so he choked up on the club.

"Up yours, Jay," he yelled back and started to swing. As his weight shifted on the backswing, his right leg plunged almost up to the knee in the muck and he lurched to the left, flinging the club toward the ball.

Somehow, the wedge made contact as Misky's left knee disappeared in the thick soup and the ball plopped into the mud two feet away.

"I saw that! That's a stroke, you know!" Jay yelled.

Misky howled as the quicksand rose to his groin. "I can't move my legs! Get me out of here!"

"Are you going to take a drop?" Jay hollered back. Misky's belt disappeared below the surface.

"Forget the ball! Get me out of here!" he shrieked.

"It'll cost another stroke, you know!" Jay called. The muck bubbled over the little green alligator logo on Misky's shirt.

"Help! Lift me out!" he cried.

"No clean and lift!" Jay yelled back. "No winter rules at this club, Misky!" The quicksand oozed toward Misky's chin as he waved his arms over his head.

"Please, somebody! Caddie! What's your name? Sully! I'll double your tip!" The muck filled his mouth and his eyes bugged out just before his head disappeared into the ooze.

Sully's headache had finally faded away. He had paid the full price for last night's unfortunate escapade and the red haze on the back of his eyeballs was gone, too. Now all he felt was tired. His shoulders were a little sore, too. He did, however, have a new appreciation for Mr. Jay.

"Mind if I leave his clubs here, Mr. Jay?" he said. "They're heavy."

"Why don't you just leave them over there with him, Sully?" Jay answered. "Then hurry up so I can putt out. I think you'll need to tend the pin." Sully handed him his putter.

Sully stepped over the creek and took two squishy, careful paces through the mud. Then he heaved Misky's oversized bag in the general direction of the man's ball. They landed with a satisfying splat and began to sink into the muck next to Misky's pitching wedge, which slowly sank from sight clenched in his cold, cheating hand.

Superhero Grudge Match

Batman made a big show of checking the Bat Watch when Superman swooped to a landing behind the first tee at Pebble Beach.

"Sorry," Superman said as he extracted his golf clubs from beneath his cape and handed them to his caddie. "Lois got stuck in the elevator at the Daily Planet and I had to pull the building apart to get her out."

Batman smirked. "For a superhero, you are seriously hen-pecked."

Superman pulled on a golf glove and flipped him the bird. He wasn't going to let the Caped Crusader's ragging distract him from his game. The match was too important.

The winner would represent the Justice League in the AT&T Championship Pro-Am, a singular honor for the superhero who won the right to play in the tournament and a key element in the League's PR effort to modernize its image and extend its brand to new audiences. It was also literally singular because the Justice League could only afford the entry fee for one player. On-line games and other digital competition was killing their bread-and-butter comic book business.

From the look of things, times were tough in the old Bat Cave, too. Superman noticed Batman's cape was kind of frayed around the edges— it might even be last year's style. He wasn't surprised. He'd heard rumors that Bruce Ward's fabulous fortune had suffered under the kind ministrations of Bernie Madoff. That might also explain why the Dark

Knight didn't hire an experienced Pebble Beach caddie for the round. Robin the Boy Wonder was toting the Bat Bag.

Superman nodded to Robin, then introduced himself to Larry Linwood, a rising star on the PGA Tour and a devoted comic book fan. The winner of today's match would be his celebrity playing partner in the tournament.

"It's a real honor to meet you, Superman," Linwood said. "I don't read much, but when I do, it's a comic book." Linwood, 23, was the TV spokesman for the largest investment bank in America as well as the world's leading skateboard manufacturer. He had won three times on the PGA Tour since dropping out of his freshman year at Mid-Nevada State University to turn pro, which also qualified him to own a beachfront home in Malibu and a Maserati. He normally skipped the AT&T to play for a rumored million dollar appearance fee in Papua, New Guinea, but the prospect of playing alongside a superhero outweighed his agent's greed this year. "When I found out I was going to play with one of you two guys," he said to the two crime fighters, "I almost wet my pants."

"Hey! Hold it down back there! I'm trying to play some golf here!" It was Bill Murray getting ready to tee off ahead of them. He was playing a practice round with D.A. Points, the pro with whom he'd won the pro-am the year before. "And lose the capes," he added. "This is a class joint. Sheesh!"

Batman waved an acknowledgement as the Boy Wonder exclaimed, "Holy gopher guts, Batman! That's Carl Spackler!"

"Now fellas," Linwood said as they walked onto the tee to wait for Murray's group to play their second shots, "the only thing you've got to remember is that we have to play by USGA rules."

"So that means no faster than a speeding bullet and no leaping tall bunkers in a single bound, right?" Batman said, staring directly at Superman.

"And no Bat Drivers or Bad Wedges or any other Bat Crap," Superman replied.

"Uh, yeah," Linwood said. He hoped he wouldn't have to break up any fights between the two obscenely muscled men. "I'm not going to play, just watch and kind of referee. So let's have a fair match, okay?" He tossed a tee in the air. When it landed he said, "Batman, you have the honors."

In a classic case of first tee jitters, neither superhero did well on the first hole. Batman hit driver KABOOM! against the advice of Robin, who pointed out it was a short hole that punished a slicer, which Batman definitely was. Superman cold-topped his tee shot DRAT! and was lucky to tie the Caped Crusader with a double bogey.

"That's all right, boys," Linwood said. "There's plenty of golf to be played."

The second hole was a different story. Batman's approach was blocked by the tree on the left, but Superman hit a miracle hybrid KERSMACK! out of the right rough and chipped in for a three from the back of the green.

"Eagle!" he cried as the ball hit the flagstick CLANK! and dropped to the bottom of the cup.

"Sorry Superman," Linwood laughed. "We play this hole as a par four during the tournament. It's a great birdie, though."

Overly excited, the Man of Steel barely held the honors with a bogey on three, but he was still one up when they came to the fourth tee.

"Keep it in the fairway here, boys," Linwood advised. "And watch out on the right for the big water hazard called the Pacific."

Superman's drive was short but in the left center of the fairway. One up and feeling cocky, he said, "Top that, Bat Ears," and winked at Batman as he picked up his tee.

Fuming, Batman fumbled for a ball. Skin-tight leotards made it tough to carry balls, tees, ball markers, and divot tools. Nor did it help that he'd put on a couple of extra pounds over the holidays. When he finally extracted a ball from the pocket in his tights, he took extra care teeing it up, aligning the Bat Logo just ever so. Batman took a mighty swipe at the ball and KERBLAM! Anger fueled his swing, not to mention his slice.

"Holy banana ball, Batman!" exclaimed Robin as the errant ball sailed toward the ocean.

Unperturbed, Batman adjusted his glove, surreptitiously turning a hidden dial on its cuff. His ball immediately swerved left and spun back onto the fairway some thirty yards beyond Superman's.

"What was that! I thought there wasn't going to be any of that Bat Baloney," Superman protested.

"What baloney?" Batman said with wide-eyed innocence, an expression very hard to pull off when the top of your face is covered by a mask.

"Are you going to allow that?" Superman demanded of Linwood.

The pro grimaced and shrugged. "The wind off the ocean can help you or hurt you." The Dark Knight chuckled as he strode off the tee.

As soon as they were on the green, Batman marked his ball and tossed it to Robin, who wrapped it in this towel and gave it a vigorous cleaning.

"Let me see that ball," Superman demanded, holding out his hand to the caped caddie.

Robin looked at Batman for instructions. The crime fighter nodded. The Boy Wonder handed the ball to Superman, who examined it closely.

"None of that X-ray vision stuff, now," Batman cautioned.

Superman didn't bother. He was sure Robin had switched balls in the towel anyway. His suspicions were confirmed when he noticed an extra bulge in Robin's Speedo as the Boy Wonder tended the pin. He didn't point it out, though, because there was an unwritten superhero rule about checking out each other's loads.

When Batman made his two-putt par and Superman, still furious, missed his, the match was all square. It stayed that way as both superheroes bogeyed the fifth and double-bogeyed the sixth holes.

"You know, I normally play better than this," Batman whispered to Linwood as they trudged to the seventh tee.

"I'm sure," Linwood said. "But don't worry. You guys will play at your handicap during the tournament. What's yours, by the way?"

"I'm a five," Batman said. Superman snorted. "What's yours, Stooper Man?" Batman demanded.

"Four," Superman said. "What's it to you?" Batman just shook his head.

Linwood's heart sank. He knew how much damage a vanity handicap could do in tournament play. No matter which one he chose, he'd be carrying them the entire round. And they were both pretty beefy.

"Okay, Mr. Five," Superman said as they reached the seventh tee. "You're up."

Photographs don't do justice to the majesty and danger of the seventh hole at Pebble Beach. The Pacific crashes against the rocks on two sides of the green while the player stands a mere hundred yards away— and nearly twenty yards above it—trying to decide whether the wind calls for a soft, floating half wedge or a low punched five iron. Meanwhile, seagulls fill the air and sea lions cavort in the surf. What matters most, though, is the wind. How strong is it? Where is it coming from? Above all, where is it going to send your ball?

After a lengthy consultation with Robin and much tossing of grass into the air, Batman decided the wind was slightly against him so he pulled a nine iron. Superman thought Robin gestured toward his crotch where the Bat Ball was hidden, but Batman almost imperceptibly shook his head and teed up a regular ball.

Batman's swing was far from picture perfect, but the ball rose lazily in the air and arced toward the pin. As the ball reached the peak of its flight, Superman noticed Batman holding the finish of his swing as if he were posing for *Golf Digest*. That was too much. The Man of Steel coughed, ostensibly covering his mouth with his fist but actually directing a jet of Super Breath WHOOSH! at Batman's ball as it started to fall to earth. The ball flew over the green and KERSPLASH! it plunged into the Pacific.

Batman dropped his pose and whirled to confront Superman. "Cheat! You cheat!" he shouted.

Superman smiled. "The wind off the ocean can help you or hurt you," he said. "I think I heard that somewhere before."

Batman sputtered and slammed his club down into his bag, but didn't say anything else while Superman punched a seven iron under the wind to the front of the green. Even after he three-putted for a bogey, Superman won the hole.

On the eighth tee, Linwood decided he better try to ease the tension between the superheroes. "Did you hear the one about the priest, the rabbi, and the nine-year-old caddie?" he asked. Superman nodded but didn't look up from the yardage book he was studying. Batman didn't respond at all. Linwood tried some small talk.

"So Batman, I bet the taxes on the Bat Cave are a real killer, huh?" he said.

Batman gave him a dead fish stare and said. "I wouldn't know. I have people who handle that."

"Must be nice to be born with a silver spoon in your ass," Superman snarked.

"Just shut up and hit," Batman snarled.

Both superheroes kept the ball in play on the blind tee shot on the eighth hole and Superman laid up safely left of the green. Batman, still smarting from the crack about his inherited wealth, not to mention the ball in the ocean on the last hole, sized up the forced carry from the cliff edge to the tiny green on the other side of Stillwater Cove and told Robin to give him his five wood.

"That's a daring play," Linwood remarked.

"Only wimps lay up," Batman said while staring directly at Superman. He took Robin's towel and pretended to wipe off the grip of his five wood. Under the towel, he twisted the grip until the Bat Gyro clicked into place. He tossed the towel to Robin, took careful aim, and SMASH! the ball flew straight and true. CLANK! the ball hit the flagstick on the fly and landed on the back of the green. Bill Murray, standing on the ninth tee, turned around and applauded at the sound.

"Holy pin smack, Batman!" Robin cried.

Batman gave Superman a square-jawed smirk and said, "Silver spoons buy lots of golf lessons."

The Dark Knight had a tough downhill putt on the slick green. He sent the ball well past the hole and missed the come-backer, but his bogey still won the hole when Superman chunked his chip and two-putted for a double.

Batman held his slim lead through the tough ninth and tenth, tricky eleventh, and impossible par three twelfth hole. Neither player made a par on any of them, reminding Linwood why he avoided pro-ams whenever possible.

Superman eeked out a win on the thirteenth hole by virtue of a fortunate flub of his second shot, which left him below the hole on the treacherous green. Batman's second shot was even shorter, but he tried to make a heroic chip SKULL! and hit his ball off the back of the green instead. Superman followed his caddie's advice, played his chip to three feet below the cup and sank the par putt.

"Now, that's what I'm talkin' about," Superman crowed as he plucked his ball from the cup.

"Holy hambone, Batman!" Robin groaned.

Batman snorted, "Yeah, the guy makes a par and all of a sudden he's George Lopez."

Neither player could get out of his own way on the next three holes, so the match was still tied when then got to the iconic seventeenth hole. As they waited for Bill Murray and his partner to clear the green, Batman said, "So, Superman, how long was Lois trapped in the elevator?"

"About an hour," Superman answered.

"That must have been scary. Anybody else in there with her?"

"Jimmy Olsen," Superman said. "They both came out none the worse for wear after I took the building apart so the rescue team could get to them."

"I bet Jimmy was smiling," Batman said with a sly smile of his own. "How about Lois?"

"What do you mean?"

"Think about it, Supe. All alone in close quarters. A babe like Lois and Jimmy Olsen, a walking teenage penis. Both of them all hot and sweaty. Probably dark in there, too. Who knows what could happen."

Superman's face turned the color of his cape. "Up yours!" he sputtered.

"I'm just saying. . ." Batman smirked. "By the way, I think you've got the honors."

Superman glared at the Dark Knight. His caddie laid a calming hand on his shoulder, but Superman shook it off and snapped, "What's it playing?"

The caddie checked the wind and pin position and handed Superman a five iron. "Aim for the right side," he said. The seventeenth hole can bring grown men to their knees, he knew. The wind plays havoc with most shots and the treacherous peanut-shaped green is fronted by massive bunkers and split by a ridge that runs from front to back. The safe shot is to the apron on the right front, especially for a player whose nerves of steel were twanging like over-tuned guitar strings. Superman's hand shook as he teed up his ball.

Trying to be helpful, Linwood said, "Think positive, Superman. Just visualize Jack Nicklaus hitting the pin on this hole to win the US Open."

But Superman couldn't erase the mental picture of Jimmy Olsen and Lois Lane pressed together in the dark elevator. He stole a glance at Batman grinning behind him on the tee. That didn't help.

Furious, Superman WHAM! crushed the ball. Literally. He hit it so hard his ball exploded BAM! into dust.

"AARGH!" he yelled. The Man of Steel reared back and flung his five iron at the Pacific. It disappeared over the horizon.

"Holy hothead, Batman!" Robin cracked as the Dark Knight rolled on the ground in laughter.

Linwood shook his head. "I, uh, don't know how to score that. I guess it's lost. Better re-tee."

Batman picked himself up and, still laughing, drilled his shot into the front bunker.

Superman took several deep breaths and calmed down enough to hit to the right front of the green. He had a long and probably impossible bogey putt.

Batman and Robin snorted and giggled like Beavis and Butthead as they walked to the green. The laughter stopped abruptly, though, when they saw Batman's ball buried under the lip of the bunker.

"Holy barf ball, Batman!" Robin moaned. "What are you going to do now?"

Linwood peered into the bunker and shook his head. The ball wasn't just buried in the bunker face. It was lodged beneath overhanging grass that completely blocked any upward movement. "I don't think you can even get a club on it to play it out backwards," he said. "If I were you, I'd take an unplayable lie."

"I can do that?" Batman asked.

"Sure, as long as you drop in the bunker," Linwood said. "It will cost you a stroke, though."

Batman looked at Superman's position and chuckled. "Not a problem," he said. He dropped a ball in the center of the bunker, pitched out to a foot from the hole like he knew what he was doing, and marked his ball. As he straightened up, he grinned at Superman, who was standing over his ball on the right front of the green. "All you have to do is make that sixty footer for a tie," Batman snickered.

"Shake it off," Superman's caddie advised. "You can't let him get to you again. Besides, this putt's not as hard as it looks. Just hit the top of the ridge right at the apron and the ball will feed down to the hole."

Superman took three practice strokes and rapped his ball firmly. It wasn't firmly enough, however. The ball rolled exactly to the right spot at the top of the ridge, but trickled too slowly toward the cup. As it stalled on the rim, Superman THUMP! stomped his foot. The tremblor measured 3.4 on the Richter scale at the Northern California Earthquake

Data Center in Berkeley. Trees shivered and startled birds took to the air all over the Monterey Peninsula. KERPLOP! Superman's ball tipped into the hole.

"Yours is good," Superman said as the smug smile faded from Batman's face.

"That can't be legal!" Batman protested.

"Why not? I didn't touch the ball," Superman said.

Linwood looked totally confused. Doubtfully, he said, "Rub of the green?"

The match was square. Batman fussed and fumed all the way to the eighteenth tee. As Superman peeled the head cover off his driver, Batman whispered to Robin. The Boy Wonder rummaged around in the bag until he found a small package about the size of a candy bar. He handed it to the Caped Crusader, but kept his eyes on Superman the whole time.

"What's that?" Superman asked. He didn't like Robin's shifty look.

Much too casually, Batman said, "Just a little energy snack. Want some?" He peeled back the bar's thick, heavy wrapper. A green glow filtered out.

Superman gasped. He dropped his driver and grabbed his throat. "Kryptonite!" he croaked.

"Heh, heh, heh," Batman cackled. "Let's see one of your super drives now!"

SLUMP! Superman dropped to the ground. He reached beseechingly toward the Caped Crusader.

"I think the Man of Steel is conceding," Batman said.

"Holy death throes, Batman!" snickered Robin. "Looks to me like he's a goner."

"Aw come on, guys," Linwood said. "There may not be a rule to cover this, but it's going to really screw up my endorsement deal with Nike if I'm playing with Superman when he dies on the eighteenth tee."

Batman considered the consequences. The Justice League had pulled a lot of strings to beat out a thousand other applicants to get one of the forty amateur slots in the tournament. And, after the miserable showing for the Captain Marvel and Green Lantern movies, not to mention the debacle of Spiderman on Broadway, which reflected badly on them even though he wasn't part of the League, the organization needed a big marketing boost. Batman thought about it as he watched Superman wriggle on the ground like a slug covered with salt.

Reluctantly, he folded the lead wrapper around the bar of Kryptonite and tossed it to Robin. "Keep that handy," he said. "You never know when he's going to get out of hand."

Slowly and in much pain, Superman got to his feet. His skin had a green tint and his tights hung loosely on his shrunken frame. He waggled his head like a boxer shaking off a roundhouse punch but his eyes cleared as he stretched his arms out and took in a huge gulp of fresh air. He picked up his driver, shook his cape out of the way, and glared at Batman.

"Watch this, Bat Bitch," he snarled.

Superman's mighty drive started directly at the middle of the fairway but soon hooked left on a trajectory in the ocean. Faster than a speeding bullet, Superman SPLASH! plunged into the water and came up with a boulder from the sea floor at the exact spot where his ball should splash into oblivion. CLICK! his ball caromed off the rock and into the fairway. Before it landed—faster than the human eye could detect—Superman was back on the tee.

Batman's lips tightened into a thin, hard line as he eyed the water dripping suspiciously off Superman's cape.

"I need a ball, Robin," the Dark Knight said. He glanced meaningfully at the Boy Wonder's crotch.

"Oh, uh, sure," Robin said. He fumbled in his shorts, fingering one dimpled white ball after another until he found the one Batman had used on the fourth hole. He pulled it out, tossed it to Batman, and rearranged the rest of his gear in his Speedo.

Batman hit a screaming slice. Before the ball could land out of bounds, though, he tweaked the dial on his glove and watched smugly as the shot circled back to the fairway. Unfortunately, he misjudged slightly and his ball came to rest behind the trademark trees that guard the right side of the fairway. One of them was directly in his line to the green.

"Serves you right, Bat Butt," Superman said as they walked off the tee.

Superman wasn't in much better shape. His ball was in the fairway but still a long way from the green. He probably couldn't have made the par five in two anyway, but he was going to have trouble getting there in three. Against his caddie's advice, he tried to hit a driver off the deck. The result was a divot the size of New Jersey and 175 yards left for this third shot.

Batman laughed derisively as Superman flung his club to the ground but he sobered up when he lined up his own second shot. A pro would simply bend his shot around the tree, but Batman didn't have that shot. What he did have, though, was a utility belt full of Bat Gizmos. He took dead aim at the left side of the tree and swung hard, counting on his natural slice to do some of the work. As the ball flew toward the leafy obstruction, Batman flipped a trigger on his belt. WHOOSH! a wire-guided Bat Rocket shot out from near his belly button. KA-BLOOIE! the left side of the tree disintegrated in a cloud of leaves and splinters in front of his ball, which sailed through unharmed. Batman was set for an easy wedge to the green.

Superman gnashed his teeth at the flagrant violation of the no-superhero-stuff rule, but his caddied calmed him down. "You can make this shot," he said. "It's right in your wheelhouse for a smooth five iron." Unfortunately, the caddie had forgotten that Superman's five iron was on the bottom of the Pacific near Hawaii.

"Hard six?" Superman asked.

The caddie remembered the exploding ball on seventeen and emphatically shook his head. "Just hit it regular. You'll make the throat on the apron. The pin is in the middle and it's an easy up and down from there." For once, Superman did as he was told and, for once, SMOOTH! pulled off the shot.

Batman responded with a SLICK! wedge of his own. His birdie putt would be long and slippery, but he liked his chances better than Superman's.

The match played out quickly. Superman CHUNK! chili-dipped his easy chip but used PUFF! his super breath to blow his ball three inches from the cup. Batman CLICK! switched on the laser guidance system in his putter and STROKE! rolled his ball perfectly. Before it could DROP! into the cup, though, Superman GLARE! fired a heat beam from his eyes and SCORCH! burned a big ball mark in its line. When the ball BUMP! bounced to the side of the hole, Batman exploded. AAARGGGH!

The Caped Crusader charged the Man of Steel like a water buffalo in heat. He hit him midsection OOMPH! The pair went down THUD! in a flurry of black and red capes. They rolled around and churned up the green TRASH! with flailing elbows and knee high super boots KICK! POKE! GOUGE! until Superman struggled to his feet. SQUASH! he clamped Batman in a bear hug and ZOOM! leapt straight up into the air. The pair disappeared into the clouds. PFFFT!

Linwood, Robin, and Superman's caddie stood speechless on the devastated green. They waited and waited for the duo to come back down, but nothing happened. "What goes up must come down, right?" Superman's caddie said.

"Maybe, maybe not," Robin answered. "Superman can fly in outer space."

"No kidding?" Linwood said. "How long can Batman hold his breath?"

"A long, long time," Robin said. "He's got the Bat Breather built into his cape. I saw him hold his breath all the way through a screening of the *Lord Of The Rings* trilogy. He stayed awake, too."

"There goes my super tip," the caddie said.

Linwood didn't say anything, but he wondered what kind of handicap Wonder Woman carried.

Choker

Alfred Bender sat alone in the club grill room contemplating the pool of grease coagulating around his cheeseburger and trying to decide how best to kill Mike Zacarelli. Alfred looked up from his half-eaten lunch to glare across the room at his intended victim holding court before a bunch of cronies who guffawed at his every word. Alfred was sure most of the jokes Zacarelli told were at his expense. He simply had to kill the obnoxious son-of-a-bitch.

He regretted not having done it on the golf course that morning. The urge struck him on the first hole when he met Zacarelli for their match in the preliminary round of the club championship. Last year, Alftred had advanced all the way to the semi-finals before encountering an over-qualified sixteen-year-old who soundly thrashed him before going on to win the trophy. This year, Alfred had spent weeks honing his game, practicing as much as playing, spending hours on the putting green and even investing in an instructional round to work on strategy with the club pro. He felt at the top of his game when he took the tee this morning. Then Zacarelli showed up.

"Great day for a game," Zacarelli said as he extended his hand. "Are you ready to rumble, Alfie?"

Alfred grimly smiled and shook the extended hand, resisting the urge to grind Zacarelli's knuckles in his grip. He hated being called anything other than his perfectly good given name. What's wrong with "Alfred?" he thought. He often had to live with "Al," although only insensitive louts like salesmen were the only ones ignorant enough to call him that. But he absolutely hated "Alfie," the Michael Caine movie notwithstanding. There was no dignity, no respect in the diminutive. Only a boor like Zacarelli would call him that.

"Do you mind," Alfred said. "I prefer 'Alfred.'"

Zacarelli looked at him blankly for a moment. "Sure," he said with a shrug. He took a tee from his pocket and tossed it between them. When it landed, it pointed at his feet. "Guess I'm the lucky one," he said. "Play well, Alfie."

Alfred winced.

Zacarelli took a five iron out of his bag and took a couple of practice swings. He teed up his ball, walked behind it to check his line, then stepped up and hit it down the middle of the fairway. It was a very safe play on the short but severely dog-legged first hole. Alfred wasn't sure, but he thought Zacarelli smiled as he handed his club to his caddie.

Alfred usually made the same safe shot on the first hole, but today Zacarelli obviously needed to be taught a lesson. "Give me the driver," he told his caddie. He noted Zacarelli's raised eyebrows with satisfaction.

Zacarelli let out a low whistle and said, "What's this all about, Alfie?"

Alfred gritted his teeth but didn't answer. He addressed his ball, visualized the high fade he intended to hit over the tree on the corner, then swung away. Unfortunately, there was latent anger in his swing. His ball was high, all right, but the fade became a nasty slice and the ball disappeared into the trees.

"Ouch," Zacarelli said. Alfred didn't look at him, but he was sure the man was smirking now.

"Do you think you can find that ball?" Alfred asked his caddie.

"Maybe. But you ought to hit a provisional just in case." He handed Alfred his five iron.

Alfred put his provisional shot just a few yards from Zacarelli's ball, then went directly into the woods with his caddie to look for his first one. Zacarelli didn't even put up a pretense of doing the sportsmanlike thing of helping them search for Alfred's ball, walking instead directly to his own in the fairway and making a bit of a show of checking his watch as if he were timing Alfred's search. That was when Alfred next considered killing the man. It wouldn't be too hard, he thought. He could lure Zacarelli into the woods out of sight of the clubhouse—maybe by asking for permission to lift his ball off a non-existent sprinkler head—then brain him with a golf club. A seven iron would be about right, Alfred thought. As effective as a blow to Zacarelli's temple might be, though, there was no way to keep one or both of the caddies from witnessing the swing or at least hearing the satisfying "thunk." Alfred dismissed the idea and went on to lose the hole.

Being one down didn't improve Alfred's attitude, but he shook the loss off by remembering something the club pro had stressed during his playing lesson: match play is often about taking advantage of your opponent's mistakes, so it's essential to be patient and wait for them to happen. As long as you can stay within a hole or at most two holes down, you've got a chance. Alfred played his game, ignored Zacarelli as best he could, and tied the next three holes. Finally, just as the pro predicted, Zacarelli missed his par putt on the fifth hole while Alfred made his. The match was even going into the sixth hole, a tricky par three.

The 190-yard hole demanded perfect precision from the tee. The elevated green had three lobes. The front one was squeezed between two impossibly deep bunkers that also protected pins cut into either of the other two lobes. You couldn't run the ball onto the green, either, since a ridge in front would send a bump and run into one bunker or the other. To make it even harder, the green sloped so severely from back to front that a tee shot that landed above the hole made it almost impossible to stop the first putt near the cup—and it was entirely possible to putt off the green.

Zacarelli reached the tee box first and teed up a ball. He had apparently forgotten the putt he missed on the last hole that gave Alfred the honors. Alfred felt the anger rise, but stayed civil. "Excuse me," he said. "I believe it's my turn?"

Zacarelli grinned not the least bit sheepishly. "Right you are. It's your honor, your honor, as the lawyer said to the judge," Zacarelli chortled.

Alfred shook his head at the old, tired pun. Focus, he told himself. He checked the green, saw the pin centered in the front lobe between the two bunkers, and felt better. That distance, he knew, was exactly how far he hit his 23-degree hybrid. He shouldn't have any trouble making par on the hole and a birdie was a distinct possibility. All he had to do was keep his mind clear and put a solid swing on the shot.

Which is exactly what he would have done had Zacarelli not jangled the change in his pocket just as Alfred began his downswing. His club made less than perfect contact and the ball hooked piteously into the left bunker. Alfred glared at his opponent.

"What?" Zacarelli said.

"You know what," Alfred growled.

"Nope, I don't know. What's it all about, Alfie?" Zacarelli said with a trace of a smile flickering across his face. "Now, do you mind if I hit?"

Alfred stepped aside but continued to glare at Zacarelli as if trying to kill him with his eyes. His caddie had to tug the club from his hand. Alfred had it in a death grip so tight his knuckles hurt when he let go.

As Zacarelli began his pre-shot routine, Alfred considered retaliating by "accidentally" kicking over his bag of clubs during the man's swing. That would be childish, he decided. There were better ways to get even. More permanent solutions to the problem that was Zacarelli.

Zacarelli's shot put his ball on the green. It was a few feet above the hole, but Alfred thought he should have no trouble making a par. When he got to the bunker, Alfred discovered his own ball buried deep in its pitch mark in the sand. He'd be lucky to get out, much less land the ball safely onto the green.

"Tough luck," Zacarelli gloated as he walked by.

"Bite me," Alfred muttered. He made two tries to get out and onto the green before he conceded the hole.

Zacarelli held his slim lead through the ninth hole. At the halfway house, Zacarelli offered to buy Alfred a drink. Alfred refused with a curt "No thanks."

"Suit yourself, Alfie," Zacarelli said. He ordered a Bloody Mary. "Extra vodka and hold the celery," he instructed. Alfred watched in disgust as the man guzzled his drink before he got to the tenth tee. Zacarelli belched, teed up his ball, and sent a massive drive right down the center.

"Ready to concede yet?" he sneered. "Or are you going to wait until the end and choke?"

Alfred wondered if it were possible that the alcohol simultaneously improved Zacarelli's game while making him more of a jerk. He had played with many obnoxious golfers at this club and others, but he'd never been paired with a total dirtbag like this. "The match isn't over," Alfred said.

Alfred managed to land his drive in the fairway, but that was about all he could say about it. As he watched Zacarelli swagger to his ball, Alfred knew he would be lucky to tie the hole.

Unfortunately, Alfred was fresh out of lucky breaks. Zacarelli won the hole with an easy birdie. As he took his ball out of the cup, he smirked, "I believe I smell a blowout coming on."

From between clenched teeth, Alfred said, "As I said, the match isn't over."

But it was. They tied the next five holes. Alfred almost won the sixteenth hole with a chip-in that lipped out and he had a decent chance to keep the match going on seventeen but it wasn't to meant to be. His approach left him with a tricky but short downhill birdie putt while Zacarelli was more than twenty feet away. Zacarelli lagged close below the hole and declared he would putt out. He tapped in for his par, then stepped directly onto the line of Alfred's putt while he bent over to retrieve his ball from the cup.

"Hey! Watch my line!" Alfred protested.

"Opps, sorry," Zacarelli said. As he stepped away, he twisted his foot just enough to grind his spikes into the turf. They pulled up several tufts of grass that were sure to deflect Alfred's ball away from the hole.

"You can't do that!" Alfred yelled.

"Do what?" Zacarelli answered with a malevolent grin.

"That's interference! It's against the rules!"

"I don't know what you're talking about, Alfie," Zacarelli sneered. "What I do know is you've got to make this putt, so try not to choke. Oh, and don't try to repair any spike marks. That's definitely against the rules."

Alfred saw red. He took a menacing step toward Zacarelli, who raised an eyebrow but otherwise stood firm. "Going to assault me?" he asked. "There are witnesses, you know." He nodded toward the caddies.

Alfred had forgotten they were there. He appealed to them. "You saw him stomp in my line, didn't you?"

Zacarelli's caddie snuck a sideways glance at his boss before answering. "I didn't see nothin'," he said. Alfred's caddie gave an apologetic shrug and shook his head.

Zacarelli chuckled and said, "Are you going to putt or just think about it?"

Alfred knew he could play the hole under protest and appeal for a ruling after the match, but it was obvious he wouldn't accomplish anything without witnesses. He stepped to his putt, gave it a half-hearted tap, and watched it dribble away from the hole after it hit the spike mark. The match was over.

"That's too bad, Alfie," Zacarelli said. "I believe you lost."

"The rules committee is going to hear about this," Alfred said, trying to sound confident but failing to persuade even himself.

Zacarelli laughed and walked off the green toward the eighteenth hole and the path to the clubhouse. Alfred dragged himself along behind. The caddies were already halfway home, already over the hill and out of sight. As Zacarelli got to the bridge that crossed the creek in front of the eighteenth green, he burst into song. "What's it all about, Alfeeee?" he warbled off-key.

That was the last straw. As Zacarelli reached the top of the narrow bridge, Alfred roared and lunged at him, determined to knock the asshole off the bridge, jump on top of him, and drown him in the water hazard below. But Zacarelli stepped aside at the last instant and stuck out his foot as Alfred sailed by. Alfred plunged into the shallow creek with Zacarelli's guffaws ringing in his ears.

After the defeat and the dunking, Alfred should have showered and gone home, but he refused to be chased away from his own club. Sitting and staring at the congealed fat from his half-eaten cheeseburger, though, he regretted his decision as he had rued so many others during the day. He heard Zacarelli's chortles from across the room. Where was justice?

Just then, the chortles turned to a choking gag. Zacarelli's cronies at first fell silent, then jumped out of their chairs and started shouting.

"Help! Call 911! He's choking!"

Alfred watched with growing interest as Zacarelli pointed wordlessly at his throat, eyes wide with fright. One of his buddies started pounding him mercilessly on the back.

"The Heimlich! Does anybody know that Heimlich thing?!" some-one yelled.

Alfred looked around the room, empty except for the frenetic and totally helpless morons jumping up and down around Zacarelli, who was now turning blue. One of Zacarelli's buddies got behind him and threw his arms around the choking man's chest.

"Wait!" Alfred yelled. "Not like that!"

He jumped up and ran across the room. He pushed the man away and wrapped his own arms around Zacarelli from behind.

"I took a course," Alfred said. He had, in fact, taken several cours-es: economics, art appreciation, even a night class in comparative reli-gion. But none in the Heimlich maneuver.

He knew how it worked, though, so he made a fist with his right hand and cupped it with his left. All he had to do, he knew, was to put his fist under Zacarelli's ribs and pull sharply up and in, forcing the re-maining air in the man's lungs to expel whatever was blocking his air-way.

Alfred made sure to do just the opposite. He put his fist on Zacarelli's chest well above his diaphragm. Then he squeezed, slowly in-creasing the pressure on Zacarelli's ribs. He could see Zacarelli's face in the mirror behind the bar. The man's lips turned dark purple and flapped just like a fish gasping on a creek bank. Alfred tightened his grip another notch and watched Zacarelli's eyes bug out. I wonder if they'll pop out, he thought. He squeezed a little harder just to see if that would happen. It didn't, but Alfred felt something snap and Zacarelli froze for an instant. Must have cracked a rib, Alfred thought. Too bad.

Zacarelli's struggles grew weaker as his skin turned a darker shade of blue. He made a feeble effort to stand up and escape Alfred's grip, but couldn't do it. After a moment, he stopped moving completely. His head lolled to the side and his eyes rolled back until only the whites were showing.

Alfred heard faint sirens in the distance, but he didn't relax his grip. He hugged Zacarelli until he was absolutely sure the man was dead, then held on just a little longer for the pure pleasure of it. Finally, just as the emergency team rushed through the door, Alfred slipped his fist down to Zacarelli's diaphragm and yanked hard up and in. A chunk of half-chewed cheese popped out of Zacarelli's mouth and plopped onto the table. It looked remarkably like a golf ball that had been laying on the bottom of a pond for a few seasons, Alfred thought, but he didn't say so.

He stepped aside as the EMTs slapped an oxygen mask on Zacarelli's face and strapped a blood pressure cuff around his flaccid arm. After less than a minute trying to find a heartbeat, they shook their heads and packed up their gear.

"Any idea what he choked on?" one of the EMTs asked.

"That," one of Zacarelli's friends said, pointing to the clot of cheese on the table.

"Didn't come out in time, huh?" the EMT said.

"Nope, but Alfie there tried his best with the Heimlich thing," someone in the crowd said.

"I owed it to him," Alfred said. "It was the least I could do after our match this morning." He added, "By the way, I prefer 'Alfred'."

Moon Golf

"One small step for man. One giant leap for mankind." Blah, blah, blah.

Everybody remembers Neil Armstrong's famous words as he stepped from Apollo XI onto the surface of the moon. Of course, there are those who believe that the U.S. government made it all up (for whatever unfathomable reason) and what everybody saw on their television screens that July night was actually taking place on a Hollywood sound stage. I can tell you for a fact that those people are wrong. Neil was on the moon all right. I know, because I was there, too.

What was I doing on the moon, you say? Like any good caddie, I was there walking the golf course making notes in my yardage book before my player showed up for the match. As inspiring as he was that night, Neil Armstrong was basically my chauffer.

As you can see though, the conspiracy theorists are partly right. The U.S. government did hide several important facts about the events that occurred on that historic flight. There's a lot they don't want you to know about the missions that came after it, too. There are some things they just can't tell you because full disclosure would produce widespread panic, not to mention the near-certain lynching of a few public officials with low handicaps.

The secret almost got out on Apollo XIV, though, thanks to Alan Shepard and his urge to show off his prowess with a six iron. I bet you remember that, too. Like everyone else on Earth, you probably got a good chuckle out of how Alan snuck one by the high and mighty mission control team at NASA. You may even remember how upset they were at first and how they then laughed sheepishly and shrugged it off as a harmless prank. I have to tell you, they were mighty pissed. About the only thing that could have been worse from their standpoint would have been if the camera had shown me pulling that six iron out of the golf bag, wiping off the grip with my towel, and handing it to Alan in front of the gallery of extra-terrestrials who were there on the moon to watch the match.

The whole thing started when that golfing fool, Dwight David Eisenhower, the President of the United States in case you didn't know, got a message from Star Overlord Niblick, the Supreme Commander of X-99, a planet on the other side of the Milky Way somewhere. In 1956, Niblick saw the first telecast of the Masters Tournament from Augusta, Georgia, which was run by men who believed they were not only masters of golf but also masters of the universe. Niblick took exception to their high and mighty attitude, so he challenged Earth to a real golf match that would show who the actual rulers of the cosmos ought to be. The stakes would be pretty high, too. Whoever won would be in charge of civilization in the galaxy for the next millennium.

Ike wanted to play the match himself and made a pretty good case about being a war hero and everything, but Earl Warren and the other boys on the Supreme Court had seen the President on the golf course. They ruled that this was too important a match to be entrusted to an amateur, especially one who sported a fourteen handicap and hit a big banana ball off the tee. Anyway, they knew Ike was really more like an eighteen than a fourteen, since people were always giving him putts and mulligans because he was President. Dick Nixon volunteered, too, but Congress wouldn't hear of that, considering his reputation. Besides, for crying out loud, the man spent his time bowling.

Niblick suggested that a good place to play would be the far side of the moon, since there was a course there already. If you could see that course, by the way, you might recognize several of the features, like an island green surrounded by a sand trap the size of the Sahara. The bunker is so deep the sides have to be held up with wooden pilings. Pete Dye copied a lot of those course design ideas from pictures I took of the course when I scouted it for Alan. Anyway, the course on the far side of the moon was chosen but the date was left open, since the Earth had no way to get a player up there in 1956.

As you might expect, the Russians got wind of the match and tried to horn in on it. The sneaky, show-boating bastards even sent Yuri Gagarin up into space to prove that their players were superior to ours, catching everyone by surprise. Niblick shrugged and said he'd play the first guy who showed up on the tee with a club in his hand, Russian or American, and so the race to the moon began.

By that time, Ike was retired and Jack Kennedy was President. He was a pretty good golfer, but just not as public about it as his predecessor. He wasn't one to welsh on a bet, though, so JFK told NASA to get it in gear and send somebody up into space right away. They sent Alan Shepard, but they wouldn't let him take his clubs the first time because the Mercury Capsule was too small, and, besides, this was just a test flight. And, just to make sure nobody even got a hint that the flight had anything to do with golf or any other sport, John Glenn pasted a little sign on the spacecraft instrument panel, reading "No handball playing here." The bosses at NASA have always been masters of the old slight-of-hand.

As everybody knows, Alan came down with an ear infection after the flight. I gave him a pack of Juicy Fruit before he left and told him he'd need it to keep his ears open during the flight, but he didn't listen to me. Like all hotshot golfers, he thought he knew better than his caddie. I was mad, but what can you do? It's his signature on the scorecard, not mine, as we say. Alan's ear infection wouldn't go away, so Neil Armstrong flew the first moon mission so I could scout the course. Neil would have represented Earth in the match, too, except Alan was a little longer off the tee so NASA decided to put their money on him when his ear infection finally got cured. He had to promise to chew the Juicy Fruit I gave him, too.

It took a few years, but Alan and I finally got up there on the moon for the big match with Niblick. I was plenty nervous and Alan was, too, as you can just imagine. What you saw on TV was Alan warming up on the practice range. You could tell how jittery he was by how he whiffed his first swing—missed the ball completely. The second one wasn't much better; the ball just dribbled a few inches into the dust in front of him. You could hear the groans from master control on TV. What you couldn't hear was the X-99er's laughing in the gallery off camera. That made Alan mad, so he whacked that third shot like King Kong and told everybody it was going for "miles and miles and miles" in the low lunar gravity and no atmosphere. It didn't, of course. That was just more of his scratch-handicap trash-talk. The ball really only flew about two hundred yards. Not bad for a six iron, but nothing to write home about.

There weren't any TV cameras on the far side of the moon, so mission control cooled off and I got Alan settled down some by the time we got to the first tee. He really sobered up when he saw Niblick there waiting for us. The guy stood about eight feet tall and had four arms. He had a nasty gleam in his eye, too, which looked even nastier since the lone eyeball was the size of a dinner plate. Alan got into the gamesmanship right away, though. He asked me how long the first hole was, making sure he spoke loudly enough so that everyone could hear him, then he told me to give him a two iron since it was "only" seven hundred yards. Niblick blinked at that one. The big extra-terrestrial shook it off, though, and striped one almost five hundred yards down the middle of the fairway. Alan put the two iron away, pulled out his driver, and hammered it almost that far himself. The match was underway.

I could go on and on with a stroke-by-stroke description of the round, but I won't, even though it was a damned exciting match. They tied the first two holes, then Alan won the third with a birdie putt that must have been two hundred feet long and broke six times. Then he hit a tremendous approach shot on the fourth hole that put him two up. Being Alan, though, he got cocky and lost the lead by three-putting the eighth hole and trying to drive the green on the ninth. I told him to lay up to avoid a deadly seventy-two-foot deep bunker guarding the right side of the green, but it was the Juicy Fruit thing all over again.

Niblick woke up on the back nine and poured it on. He won the twelfth and fourteenth holes while Alan was still fuming about needing three shots to get out of that bunker on nine. I finally got him to shake it off and buckle down. He won the fifteenth and sixteenth holes with back-to-back birdies to even the match. One thing NASA had done right was design a really hot putter—it had a big flange with two pictures of the moon on the back of it for alignment—and Alan really made it sing.

You've got to give it to Niblick, though, he was one cool customer. He wasn't the ruler of his solar system just because he was eight feet tall and good looking—that guy had game. On the seventeenth hole, a brutal nine-hundred yard par four, he cranked his drive a good seventy-five yards past Alan's, then hit a towering five iron that flew so high I thought it might interfere with the orbit of the Apollo XIV capsule whizzing by overhead waiting for us to finish. When the ball finally landed, Niblick was left with a tap-in birdie. Alan was cool too, though, and a gamesman as well. After he missed his own birdie putt, he waited until Niblick had gone through his whole pre-putt routine and was standing over that twelve-incher ready to stroke it before Alan conceded the hole. There was a lot of grumbling from the crowd and Niblick shot Alan a dirty look with that dinner-plate eye of his, but Alan just smiled as sweet as pie through his helmet's visor and walked to the eighteenth tee. Niblick was dormie, which meant he couldn't lose the match since he was one hole ahead with one to play, but Alan wasn't backing down. A tie was as good as a win, as far as we were concerned.

The eighteenth hole was a tricky par four. Not too long—only eight hundred yards—but it demanded a perfect tee shot to a landing area narrowed by fairway bunkers on both sides, then an approach shot to a wickedly sloping green where the only hope for a make-able birdie putt was to stay below the hole, which was cut only three paces from the front edge. You couldn't go in with a bump-and-run, either, since there was a vicious bunker—a crater, really—right in front of the green.

Niblick's tee shot was perfect, not surprising since he hit a conservative three-wood. Alan being Alan, though, asked me for the driver. I tried to talk him out of it because losing the hole meant Earth would be ruled by four-armed one-eyed space monsters, but no, he had to be a hotshot and hit the big stick. He swung the driver and, sure enough, the ball almost cleared the right fairway bunker five hundred yards down the pike. Almost.

As we walked down the alien-lined fairway, you could practically taste the glee in the gallery. Their hero was sitting pretty in the middle of the fairway while the Earthling showoff had a fried-egg lie in a bunker three hundred and fifty yards from the hole. There was a spring in the normally impassive Niblick's step, which was easy to detect since it sent him bounding three feet above the surface.

Alan didn't pay attention to any of that, though. He walked up to his ball and looked at it as casually as if he were playing a Sunday round for a two-dollar Nassau and was thinking about pressing the bet. When Niblick knocked his approach shot safely on the green, leaving himself a long but near-certain two-putt, Alan just shrugged and asked for an eight iron. "Don't want to be long," was all he said. That wasn't enough club, but I kept my mouth shut for a change.

Alan's shot certainly wasn't long. It was short and landed in that bunker in front of the green. Now they were openly dancing in the gallery and Niblick was shaking hands four at a time as he took his victory march up the eighteenth fairway. It was really quite a disgusting display of poor sportsmanship. It bothered the hell out of me, but Alan was so far into the zone that I don't think he heard or saw any of it. We got to the green and he waited calmly for Niblick to putt, since he was away even though Alan's ball wasn't on the green yet. That's one of those rules of match play that people don't know about. Niblick lined up his putt casually, hit it close, then started to mark his ball. Alan just waved him away, conceding the putt. He was through playing games. Alan knew he had to hole out his bunker shot to win the hole and halve the match. Anything less meant a loss with consequences too horrible to contemplate.

Playing golf on the moon isn't like playing the game on Earth, as you can imagine. The moon has one-sixth of Earth's gravity and barely any atmosphere, which means, unless you were from planet X-99, you had to play in a bulky pressure suit with a respiration system strapped on your back and weighted shoes on your feet. Well-struck drives traveled five hundred yards and high pitch shots had hang times that could be measured in hours. One thing remained the same, though, and that was the physics of a sand shot. Alan had to hit the sand behind the ball first and let the club slide under it to "explode" the ball up onto the green. Which is exactly what he did. In the moon's low gravity and trace atmosphere, however, a cloud of anything—in this case sand—will hang in the air for several minutes obscuring everyone's vision. When the cloud of moon sand finally settled, Alan's ball was nowhere to be seen.

The gallery went crazy and pressed through the security ropes onto the green trying to get a better look. Alan took advantage of the low gravity to bound out of the bunker in one big leap and raced toward the hole. I was right behind him. Niblick got there first, though, and the story was written all over his ugly face. Alan's ball was in the hole. The match was a tie.

If the game had been held any place other than the far side of the moon, the two golfers would have gone back to another hole, the sixteenth, maybe, and played a tie-breaker. But Alan and I were running out of oxygen so more play wasn't an option. Niblick grumbled and complained and the crowd got pretty raunchy, but Alan proposed a rematch. He said that next time, though, he wanted to play someplace exotic. Someone shouted out "Mars" and somebody else cried "Saturn," but Niblick pointed out that it had taken the puny Earthlings decades to just get to the moon. If Alan wanted to play someplace exotic, Niblick said, why not Myrtle Beach?

A Not-So-Brief History Of Golf Time

Organized golf in this country more or less began in 1888 in Yonkers, NY, when a Scot named John Reid persuaded some of his buddies to whack a ball around his pasture for an hour or so. It was not only amusing, but it gave them a good excuse to sit under an apple tree and drink when they finished. At first, the course had three holes and the men shared a handful of clubs Reid had brought with him from St. Andrews in Scotland, where he became enamored of the game (not to mention the whiskey).

He also liked the moniker, "St. Andrews," so that's what he named his golf course when it became an official club with members, property, and aspirations. He also added an apostrophe, probably to avoid a pesky lawsuit.

Life was slow and golf was fast in those days. It took only about 45 minutes to play the six-hole course not counting drinking time. Today, the train speeds you from Manhattan to Yonkers in 28 minutes, but a round of golf at Reid's club will eat up half your day—if not more. Life has become a blur of racing gigabytes while golf has turned into the three-toed sloth of sports. Let's face it, something's wrong when an argyle-clad investment banker can stand on the first tee and punch a button on his smart phone to trade a bazillion peach pit futures in a nanosecond on the Indonesian Commodities Exchange, but his freshly-shaved stubble could grow into a Santa Claus beard in the time it takes him to dribble his drive 195 yards into the right rough. His Mercedes got him from Wall Street to the course in seventeen minutes, which is less time than he spends lining up his four-foot putt for bogey.

What happened? How did golf in America go from a brisk two-hour walk to an interminable five-hour slog? The answer lies in the mists of time.

The game got really slow when we tried to speed it up. Playing in foursomes seemed like a good idea, for example. Instead of two guys teeing off while two more waited for them to walk to their balls, hit them again, and get out of the way so the second duo could play, you'd have all four moving down the fairway at the same time if they all played together. You'd have twice as many players going around the course simultaneously. Brilliant!

Except it doesn't work that way. In most foursomes, four guys stand around on the tee waiting for somebody to hit. Then, on the green, three guys play pocket pool while the fourth one putts. Then all four of them tell lame jokes before teeing off on the second hole. Most foursomes look a lot like state road crews with three guys leaning on their shovels while the fourth bends over to look at the hole they're supposed to be digging.

Another improvement made to speed thing up was the invention of multiple tee boxes to accommodate players of different abilities. The problem, of course, is that the additional tee boxes always seemed to be behind the old ones so that the course could play longer for the big hitters in the club. Which included everybody. Only a wimp with zero self-esteem would set foot on the white tees. And the "senior" tees? Don't look at me. I won't play from there until my wheelchair won't make it up the hill to the blues where I teed off yesterday.

If we're going to have black tees on our courses, we should adopt a system for taking testosterone out of the selection process. Why not make everybody hit a sample drive on the first tee? They're going to take a mulligan anyway, so why not make it useful? Here's the catch: if you hit your first drive in the rough, you have to move up a tee to take your next shot. Didn't reach the first fairway bunker? Ditto. You get one chance to prove you can play from the same tees as the single digit flat bellies, so let's see what you've got, big boy. Just be prepared to pay the price.

Over time, golf evolved some elegant traditions and a few rules designed to bring order to the game and keep it moving by eliminating arguments about whose turn it is. Some of them even made sense, like the one calling for the guy farthest from the hole to hit first so the other knuckleheads don't walk in front of him and get beaned. But whose bright idea was the practice of honors on the tee? What if the guy who won the last hole isn't ready to lead off? What if he has to wait for his heart to stop racing from the excitement of carding a bogey on the last hole and the exertion of walking from the cart to the tee box? Is everybody else supposed to stand around playing with their pencils while he adjusts his pacemaker? Or what if he has to pee?

If you want to speed up the game, let the first guy who gets to the tee box hit first. If there's a tie, then use the honors system. Otherwise, the second hitter should be whoever has his glove on and his club already out of the bag. Anybody unwrapping a power bar before they hit has to go last. Except for the guy in the woods taking a pee. He's last by default.

And once you've all teed off, forget about deciding whose turn it is unless somebody is directly in the line of fire. The slowest words in golf are "who's away?" You've got one guy in the left woods, one in the right, the third guy is in a bunker, and the fourth guy still hasn't found his ball in the rough back by the ladies' tee, so what difference does it make? Somebody hit already!

Golf's traditions gave the game a permanent place in the slow lane when everybody gets to the green. "Who's away?" starts all over again. Speed putting should be the rule and whoever gets to the green first should putt first, regardless of who is farthest from the hole. Those guys aren't going to make those thirty footers anyway. If the early bird got to go first, everybody would do better simply because you'd eliminate all that tension that builds while you wait for the last guy on the green to line up, pace off, plumb bob, and re-triangulate his forty-foot bogey putt. Plus, you'd have a race to the green just to see who gets to stomp around on his opponent's line.

Yet another milestone in golf's crawl was reached when we put people in golf carts so they wouldn't waste all that time wandering aimlessly around going from shot to shot on foot. Now they wander aimlessly around on four wheels. Because that's what everybody does in a cart, you included. You lay rubber leaving the tee, then get lost on your way to the ball. Since it's in the rough, you have to drive up and down, back and forth, then around in circles for a while to find it. That is, if you didn't run over it on the first pass, which you probably did since you thought you hit it a whole lot farther. The guys in the other cart have to help, too—that's only polite.

Once you find your ball, everybody needs to wait for you to hit it, since it would be horribly poor form to go zooming away while you're concentrating on your swing and everything. That goes double for your cart partner. He can't leave because you might need another club from your bag on the cart. And he can't get out of the cart and walk to his ball twenty yards away—don't you know walking slows down the game? Besides, then he'd just have to come back to the cart to get a club.

Milestone 2-A was achieved when some genius decided that all those cart tracks in the rough were ruining the turf, so cart-path-only rules came to pass. No one thought to ask if laying six inches of black asphalt in an eight-foot-wide path from tee to green would be bad for the turf.

And, God forbid, you should walk directly from the tee to your ball. It's much faster to walk from the tee to your cart, drive 225 yards on the cart path, walk across the fairway to find your ball 35 yards back in the rough (it's pristine!), walk back to get a club, walk to the ball again (assuming you remember where it is), hit it, walk back to the cart, drive thirty yards ahead because you chunked that shot you just hit, rinse and repeat. Then start over with your cart partner's ball.

More than any other single factor in golf's history, though, the PGA Tour—specifically the televised PGA Tour—did more to impede the pace of play than the Ice Age did to slow the flow of water across Greenland.

First came Arnie, then came the crowds on the first tee. Millions of new golfers not only fell in love with the guy, they thought they could play just like him. After all, he was a regular fella, too. Shirt tail hanging out, cigarette in his fist, hair flying every which way. And he looked like he was having a great time, too, with that twinkle in his eye and cute grin on his face all the time. Nothing like Ben Hogan. He may have been a regular guy, too, but he looked like a funeral director having a bad day. And he practiced all the time! What fun is that? I wanna be like Arnie. Where's the first tee?

About the time the crowds found out they couldn't actually play like Arnie, the commentators on TV started giving them false hope. Slow mo and other gimmicks allowed them to explain just how the pros do it so the guys at home could play exactly the same way. As if. Watch carefully, folks, while Jack consults his yardage book to get the exact distance from his ball to the tuft of turf on the right front edge of the green. Now he tosses some grass in the air to test wind direction. And another to judge the speed. He consults briefly with his caddie, chooses a club, and takes a practice swing. Standing behind the ball, he visualizes the shot, picks a spot six inches in front of the ball for alignment, takes his stance, waggles while looking again at his target, then let's her fly. Perfection. That's how it's done, folks, with a careful pre-shot routine.

So everybody worked out their own pre-shot routine, otherwise known as the dance of the direction-impaired blind man. Check the GPS to see how far it is to the hole, the front and back of the green, the trap on the left, the trap on the right, and the guys in the cart up ahead getting ready to drive to the next tee. The cart girl's location is on this thing someplace, just give me a minute. Information is power, so let's get more of it.

Now toss some grass in the air. That was fun, so do it again. If you can't feel the wind in your face where you're throwing the grass, do you really think it's going to affect your ball flight? No matter. It looks cools, so do it again. No, don't do it a fourth time to check direction—look at the flag. That should give you a clue.

Now take a practice swing or two or three, but be sure to check your stance, grip, and posture every time. Then stand behind the ball and visualize your shot. Try not to visualize your lunch, the last time you hit the ball into the water from here, or the cart girl's long, smooth legs. Concentrate!

Pick a target six inches in front of your ball and pretend you're going to hit over it. Take another practice swing, find the spot again, check your stance, the alignment of your heels, knees, hips, shoulders, bifocals, and the brim of your cap with the target line. Adjust your grip, distribute your weight, look at the target, look at the ball, waggle, waggle again (it looks cool, too, just like throwing grass into the wind), look at the target again, look back at the ball, look at the ball for a long, long time. Stare at it while you remember your key swing thought—no not that one; the other one about tucking your right elbow. Now swing.

Please.

We're waiting.

The View From The Mountain

Bobby Bard's expression didn't change as Mr. Powell took yet another weak lunge at the ball. The swing—if you could call it that—sent the ball arcing to the far right side of the driving range where it joined the ever-present pile of balls beside the net that protected the cars in the lot from the wayward strikes of the slicers on the range. Powell remained upright—barely—and reached for another ball so he could do it again.

"I'm gettin' better, don't you think?" Powell said. "Last week, I couldn't reach the net."

"Uh, yeah, Mr. Powell, but remember, our target is the flag out there, not the net," Bobby said. "Aim for that and try not to swing so hard this time. Hitting it far isn't as important as hitting it straight."

"Right!" Powell said, gritting his teeth with fierce determination. Bobby noticed the man's knuckles were white.

"Wait a minute, Mr. Powell," he said. "Let's loosen our grip a bit, okay? All that tension in your arms isn't going to help."

"Right!" Powell said again. Bobby couldn't see any change in the man's grip, but didn't say anything as Powell executed another perfect lunge. This time, the ball didn't arc through the air. It scuttled across the artificial turf like a mole-seeking missile. At least it didn't slice into the net.

"There you go, Mr. Powell! Straight at the flag!" Bobby said. He made a show of looking at the clock outside the pro shop. "Gee, it looks like our session is over. See you next week at the same time?"

"You bet," Powell answered. "What should I work on this week?"

"Two things, really. First, try not to swing so hard. Second, loosen up your grip. Every time you hold a club, I want you to imagine that it's an open tube of toothpaste pointed right at your crotch. If you squeeze too hard, you're going to squirt a bit white blob onto your pants. You know what that would look like, don't you?"

Powell laughed. "Right!" he cried. "I get it. See you next week."

As Mr. Powell hauled his clubs toward the parking lot, Bobby saw his next pupil coming out of the pro shop. He muttered to himself, "I gotta get a new life."

It was 2007, the tenth year Bobby had been a PGA professional. He still gave lessons six days a week to a parade of Mr. Powells, poor souls who plowed up the sad little public course across the street with slim hope of breaking 100, much less 80. They were a good-hearted lot, for the most part, but their chances of improvement were severely impaired by years of reading golf magazines, bodies better suited to operating a TV remote than a 46-inch driver, and a penchant for following swing tips from their dentists. Since they learned golf strategy by listening to TV golf commentators, they aim for every pin, try to make every par five in two, and always go for the green out of the rough, which happens to be where they spend most of their time. Teaching them was a lot like training a pig to dance. You could give a great lesson, but the result wasn't likely to be what either one of you had in mind when you started.

The driving range where Bobby taught wouldn't win any prizes, either. When it opened during the golf boom twenty years earlier, it was a marvel of modern engineering, with artificial turf covering the entire surface, stadium lighting for night play, and a triple-deck structure with hundreds of hitting bays. The artificial turf hadn't been replaced since it was first laid down, however, and the few lights that still worked were never turned on anymore because the range closed at sundown due to lack of interest. The top two decks were long shuttered, too, and the mats on the ground floor were threadbare, so thin in some spots that you could almost see the concrete beneath.

A career spent giving unheeded—and maybe unheedable—slice cures to one Mr. Powell after another wasn't exactly what Bobby had in mind when he worked his way through the system and earned his PGA credentials. His life, he thought, was a three-foot putt short of par.

As his next pupil approached, Bobby checked his schedule sheet so he could greet the new student by name. "Mr. Astrogarth!" he said. "Welcome. I'm Bobby Bard."

"Yes you are," Astrogarth said with a grin that showed a mouthful of crooked yellow teeth. He had a full head of black hair slicked back from a high forehead. His eyes were coal black, too, and they didn't so much twinkle as glow like there was a fire smoldering behind them. He extended his hand in greeting. Bobby shook it, then quickly let go, repulsed by the hard, scaly skin.

Quickly, to cover his discomfort, Bobby said, "So, Mr. Astrogarth, I guess you want some help with your game. What can I do for you?"

"I'm sure you can do quite a lot, actually," Astrogarth said. The man's dark eyes burned directly into Bobby's.

127

Bobby blinked. "Why don't you hit a few balls so I can see your swing?" Bobby said. He was glad when the man broke off his intense stare to select an iron from his bag.

"Seven iron okay?" Astrogarth said.

"Whatever you like," Bobby replied.

They walked to the tee and Bobby poured a few balls out of the range bucket. "Let's take a look at what you've got," he said. "Do you want to warm up first?"

Astrogarth chuckled. "I think I'm hot enough."

He took a slow, controlled backswing that exploded into a vicious slash at the ball. The swing was ugly, but the ball rocketed away and bounced off the fence at the far end of the range. Bobby couldn't believe his eyes. He almost never reached that fence himself—and then only with a driver and a tail wind. It was 300 yards away.

"Very nice," Bobby said, trying to sound like he was in control. "Let's see a couple more."

Astrogarth scraped another ball into position. Again, he coiled into a slow backswing then unwound with a violent swipe. Without pause, he hit three more. All but one bounced off the fence. He looked up and gave Bobby a crooked grin.

"So, what do you think?" he asked.

Bobby shook his head. "Mr. Astrogarth, I don't know what I can teach you. Your swing won't get any style points, but it ought to produce plenty of birdies."

"So it would seem," Astrogarth said. "But, then, not everything in this world is as it seems, is it?"

"Uh, I guess not," Bobby answered.

"Exactly," Astrogarth said. "There is more to golf than hitting 300-yard seven irons. Perhaps it would be helpful if I showed you what I can do with another club."

Bobby must have turned his head or blinked, because Astrogarth was waggling another club even though Bobby hadn't seen him pull one from his bag. It was definitely a different club, though.

"What's that you're hitting now?" Bobby asked.

Astrogarth didn't say anything, but he held up the club so Bobby could see the sole. "I haven't seen anybody hit one of those for years," Bobby said.

"Ah yes, the one iron," Astrogarth said. He held it out in front of his chest and gave it a waggle.

"I remember Lee Trevino's line," Bobby said. "You should stand under that club during a lightning storm because even God can't hit a one iron."

"Mr. Trevino was quite correct about God," Astrogarth replied. "But I can."

With the same disjointed swing he'd used with the seven iron, Astrogarth crushed the ball. It cleared the fence on a rising trajectory and disappeared—literally. Bobby couldn't see it hit the ground, but it must have gone 600 yards.

Bobby was speechless.

Without pausing, Astrogarth pulled another ball into position on the threadbare mat, took the same swing with the same club, and popped the ball almost straight up into the air. It came down into the range bucket at Bobby's feet.

"D...d...did you do that on purpose? With a o...o...one iron?" Bobby stuttered.

Astrogarth smiled. "Did I say it was a one iron?" he said. He held up the club again, which now was a lob wedge.

"How did you do that?" Bobby demanded even though he wasn't sure he wanted to know.

"Just a little sleight of hand, Bobby. Any competent magician could do the same trick. It's all about showing the audience what they want to see and helping them believe it's true."

"But the golf shots! Those were real!" Bobby protested.

"Yes they were," Astrogarth said. "Now, do you think you can help me with my game?"

"Uh...I uh...there's uh..." Bobby stammered. Finally, he managed to say, "I don't think there's a single thing I can do for you, Mr. Astrogarth. You should be teaching me!"

"Funny, that's what John Daly said to me once," Astrogarth said.

"Long John Daly?" Bobby

"The one and only," Astrogarth said.

"So did you give him a lesson?"

Astrogarth laughed. "You don't think that good old boy won two majors on his own, do you?"

Yeah, but look at him now, Bobby thought to himself.

"I know what you're thinking, Bobby," Astrogarth said. "Some say I coined the phrase 'all good things must come to an end.' But Daly's run was good while it lasted, wasn't it?"

Bobby had to agree with that. Before he could say so, though, Astrogarth said, "Let's skip the rest of the lesson and go upstairs. There's something I want you to see."

Bobby couldn't put his finger on why, but he didn't think that was a very good idea. "The upper bays are closed, Mr. Astrogarth," he said. "If my next pupil caught me up there, it wouldn't set a very good example."

"I don't think that will be a problem, Bobby. Your schedule is clear for the rest of the day, isn't it?"

"Oh no, Mr. Cuppler is due in just a few minutes," Bobby said. "And the rest of the afternoon is booked solid." He picked up his clipboard to prove his point, but it was blank. He was sure there had been lessons scheduled for the rest of the day.

"Come along, Bobby," Astrogarth said. "I want to show you something you can only see from an elevated viewpoint." Astrogarth went to the stairs next to the teaching bay, removed the chain with the "Section Closed" sign on it, and started up. He still had the one iron—or whatever it was—in his hand. Reluctantly, Bobby followed.

The enclosed concrete stairway was a bit darker than the open bays, although enough light filtered through to illuminate the dead leaves gathered in the corners. Astrogarth disappeared around a landing as Bobby got to the second level, but Bobby could hear the click of the one iron on the stairs. Apparently, Astrogarth was using it was a walking stick. As Bobby stepped out of the stairway onto the third level, he caught a whiff of something on the breeze. It was like rotten eggs, but disappeared before Bobby could sniff again. Astrogarth stood in the center bay, leaning on the one iron and looking out over the landscape.

The light was different up here. The sun must have gone behind the high thin clouds because Astrogarth wasn't casting a shadow.

"Come here and tell me what you see out there," Astrogarth said.

Bobby looked in the direction Astrogarth was pointing with his one iron. He saw what he expected to see, the dingy industrial neighborhood that stretched beyond the fence at the end of the range. There wasn't much there except acres and acres of concrete-block buildings, most of them with loading docks, parking lots filled with pickup trucks and older model Chevvies, Fords, and Plymouths, and a network of streets without sidewalks. Most of the buildings were only one or two stories, so Bobby could see their flat roofs stretching away into the distance. Astrogarth's last ball was probably on one of those roofs, Bobby thought. His eye was drawn to a semi belching black smoke as it navigated a turn into one of the loading docks. Maybe that was where the stinky breeze had come from.

"What do you see, Bobby?" Astrogarth said.

"Nothing much," Bobby answered. "Old buildings and a smelly truck."

"It's not Pebble Beach, is it?"

"That's for sure," Bobby said. He'd never been to the Monterey Peninsula, but he'd seen its magnificence on television plenty of times. A friend had played there once and said it was a religious experience.

"Would you like it to be?" Astrogarth asked.

"What do you mean?" Bobby replied.

"You'll see. Just close your eyes and concentrate on what it would be like if you were the head pro at Pebble Beach or someplace like it."

Bobby started to close his eyes, but popped them open when he remembered the one iron in Astrogarth's hand. Was the guy some kind of serial killer? Maybe he'd lured Bobby up here so he could brain him with the club out of sight of the pro shop!

"Go ahead, Bobby," Astrogarth crooned. "I know what you're thinking but I'm not going to hurt you. Here, hold the club if that will make you feel safer."

"That's okay," Bobby said.

"Just think about what you want out of golf," Astrogarth urged. "You don't even have to close your eyes if you don't want to. But it will help."

Bobby did as he was told. He took a deep breath, closed his eyes, and thought about his life.

Most people assume all club pros are failed tour players, that they'd tried to make it on the professional circuit but couldn't make the grade. That description fits many of them, but not Bobby. He'd never really had a desire to tee it up with the big boys on tour. He had the game, but he knew he didn't have the competitive drive to stick it out through the mini-tours where the money is slim and the grind is intense, nor the mental discipline to compete in the big show. After considering his options, Bobby had decided early in his career that he was best suited to teaching golf instead of obsessing about his personal relationship with par every day.

Now, though, he was stuck in a crappy driving range trying to persuade Mr. Powell to loosen his death grip and swing instead of lunge at the ball. When he opened his eyes, he knew he'd see the fake turf on the range curling up at the seams and a ball picker parked to one side waiting for him to crawl into the protective cage and drive it out to gather up the balls scattered across the ground while the customers on the range tried their best to hit him. What Bobby wanted, though, was to open his eyes and see a posh country club. He wanted to give lessons to wealthy members in neatly-pressed slacks and $400 sweaters who paid him hundreds if not thousands of dollars to improve their swings. He wanted the profits from a pro shop stocked with golf shirts that cost more than his best suit and shoes that were worth more than his car. He wanted *la golf pro dolce vita*.

"Now behold your future, Bobby," Astrogarth said.

Bobby opened his eyes and saw before him not a ratty driving range surrounded by industrial blight but an immaculately manicured fairway leading to an elevated green where a flag waved picturesquely against the sky. Beyond the green lay stunningly blue water that faded into the horizon. Bobby thought he recognized the hole, but the course name escaped him.

"Where…" Bobby started to ask, but Astrogarth cut him off.

"It's where you belong, Bobby. Look over there." Astrogarth pointed to the left.

It must have been a trick of perspective, but right in front of Bobby was a columned club house with massive double doors beneath a stone lintel in which was carved "Pesaquonick Golf Club." Now Bobby remembered where he'd seen the stunning golf hole—it was the signature hole at the most prestigious club on Long Island. The National Golf Links, Shinnecock, Maidstone, and The Atlantic Club were nearby. The water in the distance was Great Peconic Bay and, if this had been more than an optical illusion, Bobby would have been able to see Long

Island Sound on the far horizon. His eyes followed a veranda to the right, where he saw another set of double doors. One of them had a tasteful plaque that said "Bobby Bard, PGA, Director Of Golf." Bobby's chest swelled at the sight.

"You deserve this, Bobby," Astrogarth whispered. "And it's all yours for the asking."

Bobby wanted it—bad. He'd earned it, too. All those years of lessons, all those clubs re-gripped, all those hours picking balls, emptying the baskets into the washing machine, then into the dispensers. More than once cleaning the toilets because the boss "forgot" to pay the cleaning company. Bobby had paid his dues and then some. He wanted to see his name on that plaque for real. But how could Astrogarth put it there? And what would it cost?

With as much negotiating bravado as he could muster, Bobby said, "Mr. Astrogarth, that's a very attractive offer. I'd be lying if I told you I wasn't interested. But, no disrespect, how can you deliver?"

"A perfectly fair question, Bobby. Let me ask you one in return: Who belongs to Pesaquonick and those other exclusive clubs? Wealthy people, right? Guys who swam in the lucky gene pool. Bankers, lawyers, Wall Street sharpies. And plenty of hedge fund managers. Those are the members, right?"

Bobby nodded and started to say, "And you..." but Astrogarth interrupted.

"Let's just say I have a close working relationship with most of them."

Bobby had no doubt Astrogarth was telling the truth. He also knew the price Astrogarth charged for his services. The big question now was, would Bobby pay it?

Astrogarth read his mind again. "You're wondering about your end of the bargain, aren't you?"

"Well, yeah," Bobby said. "Is it what I think?"

"Yes, Bobby," Astrogarth answered. "It's exactly what you think. But consider the relative value of the two parts of the bargain. Look once again at the sparkling water on the bay. What is your tiny soul compared to something like that? Besides, what good does a soul do you? You can't eat it! You can't put it in the bank! It's a trifle. A mere trifle!"

Bobby had to admit he had a point. To be perfectly honest, Bobby had never spent much time contemplating his immortal soul. Or anything else much more eternal than his car payments. Still, he felt like Astrogarth was taking advantage of him.

"I don't know," Bobby said.

"Let me sweeten the pot," Astrogarth said. "Look over there." He pointed to his left with the one iron.

Bobby could barely make out the Manhattan skyline in the far distance. Slowly the vision cleared and grew larger as if Bobby were looking through a zoom lens. In a few seconds he found himself in front of a bookstore window on Fifth Avenue. Inside was a table full of books with Bobby's picture on the cover and a giant poster proclaiming him "Golf's Greatest Teacher." A line of buyers with the books in their hands snaked through the store to another table where Bobby saw himself smiling and autographing copies.

Before Bobby could say anything, Astrogarth said, "Wait! There's more."

The bookstore window dissolved into a TV studio. Bobby saw himself in front of the cameras demonstrating a perfect golf swing. Behind him was a set with "Golf's Greatest Teacher" on the wall next to the Golf Channel logo. Bobby's heart soared.

Again, Astrogarth read his mind. "Yes, Bobby, you can be the next Michael Breed. You can have your own TV show."

"Sold!" Bobby exclaimed. Then he remembered another show on the Golf Channel, the one about John Daly's wreck of a life. "Wait! How do I know you're not going to trick me?"

Astrogarth briefly scowled, then spread a grin across his face that showed his mouthful of ugly teeth. "All right," he said. "Here's my best and final offer. One you can't refuse. I'll give you a trial period—let's say a year. If you're not happy after 365 days as Golf's Greatest Teacher, the deal is off. Of course, you'll have to leave Pesaquonick and everything else behind, but you'll be a free man. What do you say? Deal?"

Bobby didn't hesitate. "Deal!"

* * *

Everything happened just the way Astrogarth promised, although Bobby was a little queasy about some of the details. The head pro at Pesaquonick, for example, suddenly "retired" when one of his assistants threatened to sue the club for sexual harassment, which made Bobby wonder what he had gotten himself into. He shook it off, though, when he got the call offering him the job before his letter of application even had time to reach the club president's desk. Bobby soon forgot the circumstances when he settled into his plush office at the columned club-house.

Within a month after he'd started his new job, Bobby received a call from one of the editors of *Golf Magazine* offering to ghost-write not just a column in the magazine but a book for him as well. He'd heard a lot about Bobby from some of the club's members, he said, although Bobby later learned the man had been threatened with termination by the editor in chief if he didn't land a deal with "Golf's Greatest Teacher." Bobby assumed the editor in chief had one of those "close working relationships" Astrogarth had with so many people.

The book was finished in three weeks and hit the bookstores the same day the Golf Channel called. Would Bobby be interested in an hour in prime time every week? Donald Trump, for some reason, had decided to discontinue producing his golf program and they needed a replacement. Bobby knew Astrogarth definitely had his hand in that decision—who else could keep The Donald off TV? Regardless, it wasn't long before Bobby was flying to Orlando every week to tape his show.

Life was good. So was the money. Bobby's book sold like a Stephen King bestseller and his TV show topped the charts—beating not just every program on the Golf Channel but often edging out even "The Real Kardashians At Home." The pro shop at the club minted money, too. Pesaquonick members bought $200 golf shirts and $500 drivers as easily as David Feherty made jokes about Gary McCord's mustache. The members also couldn't take enough lessons. Bobby charged a full $600 for a thirty-minute session and much, much more for a three-hole playing lesson, but his calendar was always full. The members loved him.

Once Bobby got used to the way the members flashed their money around, though, he discovered that they didn't play golf any better than Mr. Powell and his down-at-the-heels buddies back at the old driving range. Slices hit with the latest Ping wonder club went just as far right as those from a ten-year-old Callaway—even though they sailed over the cliff into Peconic Bay rather than into the sagging net in front of the driving range parking lot. And while the Pesaquonick members may have been able to pay for more lessons, they didn't practice any more than regular people, so the lessons didn't help much. Over time, Bobby found himself less and less satisfied with his decision.

About a week before the anniversary of his deal with Astrogarth, Bobby found himself on the lesson tee squinting at the screen on his video camera as Mrs. Smithson took yet another weak swipe at the ball he'd teed up for her moments earlier. It was his third lesson of the morning and his mind was wandering a bit. In fact, his brain was roaming wildly into very strange territory, which is why he was squinting at the viewfinder. When he mushed his eyelids together, he had accidentally discovered, Mrs. Smithson's withered flanks looked almost like the taunt, juicy behind of a girl thirty—maybe even forty—years younger than the moneyed dowager who had been slicing ball after ball onto the range for the last half hour.

Repulsed by the disgusting ideas the squinty view of Mrs. Smithson brought to mind, Bobby muttered, "I gotta get a life."

With more than just a hint of flirtation in her voice, Mrs. Smithson asked, "What's that, Bobby dear?"

"Oh, uh, nothing, Mrs. Smithson," he answered. "I just noticed an adjustment I'd like you to make on your back swing. Our time's about up for today, so let me show it to you on the monitor."

Bobby didn't have anything he wanted to show her, of course, but he knew he'd find something when he played the video back on the giant TV in the teaching center behind the range. Not that it would make any difference in the old lady's swing. He'd been giving her lessons every week for the last four years and she still couldn't hit a golf ball much farther than she could throw her dead husband, the hedge fund mogul who left her the membership at Pesaquonick along with a simply immense pile of municipal bonds bought with the profits of gambling on the stock market with other people's money.

Inside the learning center, Bobby plugged his video camera into the 48-inch TV so he could show Mrs. Smithson her many swing flaws in all their cinematic glory. The high-definition monitor also gave him an up-close-and-personal view of the woman's neck wattles, wrinkled arms, and Botoxed forehead that he couldn't squint away. As he remembered his indecent thoughts about her on the range, Bobby decided he'd been out in the sun too long.

"Don't you think I'm playing better, Bobby?" said Mrs. Smithson, interrupting his reverie. "I almost got a par last week on the fourth hole!"

"That's wonderful, Mrs. Smithson," Bobby answered. "I really think you're on the verge of a breakthrough." He fiddled with the controls on the TV. "Now, I want you to look at your swing on the monitor. See how your left wrist is cupped at the top of your backswing?

That's what causes your slice." He rolled the video while the woman started intently at the screen.

"Oh yes! I see exactly what you mean," she purred. Bobby was sure she didn't have a clue as to what he was talking about. He was also sure she had something else on her mind besides proper wrist pronation.

Before he could point it out to her, the phone in the learning center rang. It was the assistant in the pro shop telling him his next lesson was here. Bobby told him to send the student down to the range. He hung up the phone and turned to Mrs. Smithson. "Let me see your left hand, please," he said. "This week, I want you to work on keeping your wrist bowed like this." He bent the hand gently downward. "Keep it in this position all the way through your swing. Will you practice that for me?"

When he let go of her her hand, she let it fall to his hip. "I promise, Bobby dear."

"Good. I'll see you next week," Bobby said, sliding away from the hand that was creeping around from his hip to his butt. His career, he decided, was still one Titleist short of a dozen.

Bobby smelled his next pupil before he saw him. A whiff of sulfur greeted him as he came out of the teaching center to find Mr. Astrogarth leaning casually on his one iron on the lesson tee. The man's face split into a grin that showed an amazing number of crooked yellow teeth.

"Bobby my boy! So good to see you!" Astrogarth said.

"Hello, Mr. Astrogarth. I, uh, was expecting Mr. Doltwater. He's scheduled for a lesson today."

"George Doltwater sends his regrets, Bobby," Astrogarth said. "Unfortunately, his Bentley hit a mis-placed cow on his way to the club.

Doltwater is fine, but he's busy right now negotiating with a farmer over damages. Knowing Doltwater, he'll end up with another investor for his hedge fund and a freezer full of hamburger. Anyway, I didn't think you'd mind if I took his place. In fact, I thought you'd be glad to see me."

"Actually, I did want to see you, Mr. Astrogarth." Bobby wasn't sure how to start, but he was pretty sure he wanted to cancel his deal. He wasn't too concerned with his soul, but he didn't like the view of his future when he squinted at Mrs. Smithson.

"Let me guess," Astrogarth said. "I bet you've found that being head pro at a wonderful place like this isn't all it's cracked up to be. Am I right?"

Tentatively, Bobby nodded.

"Even if it could lead to even better things? Like your name on the pile of municipal bonds in Mrs. Smithson's account? That can be arranged, you know."

Bobby shuddered. "No thanks, Mr. Astrogarth."

Astrogarth chuckled. "I didn't really think so. But before you make up your mind completely, let's go visit the third hole. The view there is lovely."

Not again, Bobby thought, but he got in the cart with Astrogarth anyway.

Pesaquonick was built on an old, abandoned farm on eastern Long Island where the land had been shaped by glaciers, then polished by wind and water over subsequent eons. The third tee was built atop the high point on the course, Hurricane Hill, where local Indians were rumored to have watched for approaching storms in the days before white men pushed them off the land and into the casino business. The views were spectacular. To the south was the Atlantic Ocean, to the north Great Peconic Bay and Long Island Sound, and on a really clear day you could just about make out a smudge of the Manhattan skyline to the west. Hurricane Hill was Bobby's favorite spot on the course. Lately he seemed to find himself there often, contemplating life and trying to get at the root of his discontent. He wondered if Astrogarth knew that.

"Now close your eyes, Bobby. You know the drill." When Bobby's eyelids fell, Astrogarth added, "I want you to imagine what it would be like if you had only one pupil—but he was the best golfer in the world. It would be match made in...well, never mind where. It would be a dream team of golf's greatest teacher and the game's greatest player."

Bobby began to salivate.

"Now behold your future."

Bobby opened his eyes and saw someone on the lesson tee in the distance. The man was tall and muscled, his skin dark, his swing elegant. Bobby watched him hit one perfect shot after another, sending the ball high, then low; left, then right, each shot obviously coming to earth exactly where the man wanted it to land. Bobby knew who it was.

"Yes, even he needs a coach, Bobby. He's god-like in his perfection, but it's early in 2008 and, between you and me, he's not going to finish the year in a blaze of glory although you might want to bet heavily on him to win the US Open. When he recovers from the surgery that's coming, he's going to want a new coach."

"But..." Bobby tried to say, but Astrogarth interrupted.

"Just think of it, Bobby. One pupil—and one who can actually find his way around the golf course without GPS on his cart. Your relationship with him will be a vastly different from that with your current pupils. Also the rewards. Hitch your wagon to Tiger's star and there's no telling where you'll end up."

Bobby knew Tiger's swing coach had it made. There would be practice sessions shielded from the press but surrounded by agents, secretaries, and gophers waiting on him hand and foot. He would fly first class (or maybe even in Tiger's private jet) to tournament sites around the world just to be there in case the man needed some advice. Who knew, maybe he'd even become like part of the family, chumming around with Tiger's wife and kids, hanging out in the mansion in Florida. As Bobby looked into the future, Tiger waved to him from the Pesaquonick lesson tee. Bobby blinked, and the vision disappeared.

"That future looks pretty good, doesn't it?" Astrogarth said.

"Yes, it does," Bobby agreed, but then he slowed himself down. "But what's the catch?"

"Catch! Bobby, I'm offended!" Then Astrogarth smiled disarmingly. "Not really. My hide's pretty thick. But my word is as good as gold. I held up my end our last deal, didn't I?" Bobby had to agree.

"Of course, a few things will change. You'll have to resign from Pesaquonick and give up the TV show." He hurried to add "But the money will be fabulous. What do you say? Deal?"

Bobby wanted to shout "yes!" but instead said, "Not so fast, Mr. Astrogarth. Isn't my soul still on the line here?"

"Well, yes. That almost goes without saying. Not quite without saying, but almost."

"Can I have another trial period?" Bobby asked, even though he knew the answer.

144

"Sorry Bobby, one to a customer." Astrogarth winked and put his arm around Bobby's shoulders. "This is an offer that won't be repeated, my friend. Do we have a deal?"

Bobby swallowed hard, but he agreed.

Astrogarth beamed. "Bobby, just to show you what kind of guy I am, I'm going to do you a big favor. You've saved up some money from your year here at Pesaquonick, haven't you? And you'll be making boat-loads more with Tiger, so let me introduce you to someone to help you manage your money."

"Gee, thanks, Mr. Astrogarth," Bobby said.

Astrogarth handed him a business card. "Just call this number and tell them I vouch for you. I work closely with the principals of the firm."

Bobby looked at the card and asked, "Who should I speak to?"

Astrogarth smiled his crooked yellow-toothed grin and said, "Just ask for Bernie Madoff."

Night Putting

Denny and Marvin stood on the fifteenth tee, trying to follow the flight of a tee shot as it disappeared into the dusk.

"I think I saw it bounce," Denny said. "Right edge near the one-fifty marker."

"Nice shot," Marvin said.

"Thanks. Think we'll finish the round?"

"Sure," Marvin answered. "Don't we always?"

A threesome had played through them some time ago and were probably putting out on the eighteenth green in what little light was left. Denny and Marvin would soon be the only humans on the course.

The creatures of the night would be appearing, though. Denny and Marvin were used to watching the deer step tentatively from the woods at twilight to nibble the succulent grass in the rough. Occasionally, they crossed paths in the dark with a coyote meandering across the fairway or heard a raccoon splashing in the creek that wound through the course. Last week, as they approached the seventeenth green where the dark woods crowded the fairway, they heard a loud SLUUURP in the woods.

"Gross!" Denny said. "What the heck was that?"

Marvin peered into the blackness, but couldn't see anything moving in the trees. "Swamp gas, maybe?" he offered. They played on.

Tonight, in terms of humans on the course, Denny and Marvin were all alone.

They strode purposefully off the tee and soon found both drives in the fairway. Neither player was a long hitter, which can be an advantage when it comes to finding your ball in the dark. The flag fluttered dimly in the distance. In a few more minutes, it wouldn't be visible at all from where they stood. Marvin's approach shot looked good as it left the club and he expected to find the ball on the putting surface. Denny, though, caught his a little thin. When he last saw it, it was heading for the bunker to the left of the green.

Denny and Marvin were twilighters, devout golfers who give up their after-work cocktail with the gang from the office and often even dinner with their loving wives and children in order to play golf in the hours before (and sometimes immediately after) sundown. They find pleasure searching the fairway for balls hit straight but lost in the gloaming, or putting on the last two holes by flashlight. They can't ride a cart because the garage underneath the clubhouse would be closed when they bring it back.

Most twilighters don't care about the inconveniences because they play for the pure love of the game. Denny and Marvin, though, played at twilight not just because they were dedicated golfers, although they were, but also because they were cheap. That's one of the big advantages of playing late in the day: twilight rates can be half of the normal-hours greens fees. If you appreciate the value of a buck, it's well worth it to play your round while the sun sets, the darkness gathers, and the mosquitoes and other blood-sucking creatures of the night rise from the woods lining the fairways.

Denny was surprised to find his ball on the green. There was a track through the sand, so it must have skipped through the trap, although he didn't think it had been hit hard enough to do that. The trail through the sand didn't look normal, either, but sometimes the fading light played tricks on you. He just thanked his lucky stars the ball was on the green and marked it so he could clean it. He picked it up only to discover the ball was covered with a film of clear slime. Then he saw puddles of the same stuff spotting the green around his ball marker. "Yech," Denny said as he wiped his ball on his towel. He replaced it and took his time putting out.

Denny and Marvin violated one of the cardinal rules of sundown golf, irritating the other denizens of the dusk to no end. They refused to sacrifice the rules of the game on the altar of speedy play. Twilighters flirt with darkness whenever they tee off, and it's a matter of pride that they play every single hole before it becomes too dark to see the ball at their feet. Consequently, twilighters tend to lose a lot of balls because it takes so much time to look for them. They often concede otherwise-difficult putts because they can't read the line anyway. And they don't dawdle when it's time to swing the club. Not Denny and Marvin, though. If a tee shot settled down unseen into the rough somewhere, they spent the full allotted five minutes looking for it. Rules are rules, you know. Besides, balls are expensive. They didn't play ready golf, either. They adhered to the customs of "honors" and "away." And they never, ever conceded a putt. The hole was not over until the ball rattled to the bottom of the cup. Fortunately for the other twilighters, they didn't mind letting the more time-conscious golfers play through. That meant, of course, that Denny and Marvin were almost always the last players to walk off the course, often in total darkness. Their children often went to bed before their fathers finished the back nine and their long-suffering wives were known to drink an extra glass of wine and nod off in front of the TV before their husbands crept through the front door.

The sixteenth hole is a downhill par three. The green lies behind a creek and has traps on the other three sides. The woods crowd the bunker left of the green, with some of the big old oaks and maples hanging over the trap itself. That side of the green was effectively out of play unless, of course, that's where the hole happened to be cut that day. As near as Denny and Marvin could determine, that's exactly where it was that evening. It made no difference to Marvin; his fade/slide/banana would put his ball on the right half of the green anyway. Denny's shot looked right on target when it left the club face, but it disappeared completely in the deep dark shadows on the left side of the green.

"I think that's right on the money," Marvin said.

"All I gotta do is find it," Denny answered.

"Should be on the green. Heck, I'd look in the cup first."

But Denny's ball wasn't in the cup. In fact, Denny had to pace the perimeter of the green to find it on the back fringe. As he reached his ball, he heard some leaves rustle on the forest floor. The stealthy sound made the hair on the back of his neck tingle with the feeling that someone was watching him from the woods on the other side of the trap. He peered deep into the trees. It was so dark in the woods he could barely make out the tree trunks, much less anything behind them. He shook it off, but the feeling that someone or something was watching him overwhelmed him, and Denny yipped his putt five feet past the cup. He missed the come-backer, too, and carded a bogie.

The creek and woods continued around the seventeenth tee and lined the entire left side of the hole. From the tee, it looked like a featureless black wall just a few yards away from the edges of the fairway. Again, Marvin's tee shot zoomed to the right and away from the trees, while Denny snap-hooked his into the ominous woods about a hundred yards out.

Squinting into the gloom, Marvin saw an indistinct shape briefly emerge from the woods where Denny's ball had gone in, then disappear back into the trees. He thought he saw something, anyway. "What was that?" he asked sharply.

"What was what?" Denny had been busy pounding his driver against the ground in frustration.

Marvin looked more closely, but couldn't see anything. "Nothing, I guess. I thought I saw something down there where your ball went."

A little shiver ran down Denny's spine at the thought. It was much the same feeling he'd had when he thought something was watching him on the last green. "What was it?" he demanded.

"I don't really know. A shape. A pale shape. Looked like it brought something out of the woods and dropped it. Then it disappeared."

Denny really hoped Marvin was pulling his leg. Bravely, he said, "Yeah, right. You're just trying to shake me up. A little gamesmanship." They walked off the tee.

"Suit yourself," Marvin said as they split up. "I'm just glad my ball's on the other side of the fairway." Uncertainly, Denny waved him off.

The creek made the rough on the left side a lateral hazard, so Denny walked to where he thought he'd seen his ball disappear, ready to drop another one. As he approached the spot, again he had a strong and very creepy feeling of being watched by something from the trees. His palms sweaty, he craned his neck trying to see into the blackness under the leaves. Glancing down, he saw a ball lying in the long grass at his feet. He tried to push thoughts of a pale creature in the woods to the back of his mind while he bent over to peer closely at the ball. It sat up perfectly—almost as if it had been teed up on a tuft of grass. It was surrounded by a puddle of slime.

Something splashed softly in the creek behind him. Denny's head snapped around, but he saw nothing. Gotta get out of here, he thought. Mentally, he declared his lie to be in standing water. He kicked his ball out of the puddle, grabbed a club, and slashed away, sending the ball in the general direction of the green. As he sprinted after it, he looked around for Marvin. He finally spotted him in the distance waiting near the woods on the left side of the green. Marvin pointed to the creek, indicating that Denny's ball had landed in it. Denny didn't care. He just wanted to play out the hole and get out of there, so he put his head down and hustled up the fairway. By the time he got to the green, Marvin was gone.

Must be on the eighteenth tee, he thought hopefully. Almost in one motion, he dropped a ball next to the creek and chipped onto the green. It was now completely dark. Only a sliver of moon and a few weak stars lit the green, but Denny saw a trail of slime leading from the creek across the green past where Marvin had been standing. It ended at the hole. Someone, Marvin presumably, had left the flag out of the hole.

"Marvin?!" Denny called. There was no answer.

He putted without even bothering to line up his twenty-footer. His ball somehow found the hole and he heard it hit the bottom of the cup. When he got there, though, it was sitting four inches away in a puddle of slime. He tapped it in one-handed and reached down to retrieve it with the other, but the ball didn't rattle into the cup this time. It made a squishy sound instead, as if it had landed in a bowl of Jell-O. Hesitantly, he reached down for it, extending his fingers toward the hole. As he did, a stray moonbeam glinted off something just on the other side of the cup. It was Marvin's putter.

He reached for the club just as a pale, slimy hand arose out of the hole. He yanked back his arm and took a step back. The hand waved his ball in the air as if trying to lure Denny closer. That wasn't going to happen.

Denny turned and ran like hell. Something behind him roared in frustration as Denny raced across the green. He ran past Marvin's cap then leaped over his partner's clubs spilled out of the bag near the cart path. He heard them clink as something ran through them after him. Out of the corner of his eye, Denny thought he saw a pile of white bones gleaming on the grass. He raced for the only light he could see, the street lamp in the parking lot. Wet footfalls squished behind him. He pounded up the eighteenth fairway leaving ball, clubs, and whatever was left of Marvin behind. Halfway through the parking lot gate and safety, something wet and heavy brushed the back of his shirt. Denny made a desperate lunge.

People who play golf at the extreme ends of the day are different from so-called normal golfers (if there is such a thing as a normal golfer). The early-morning dew chasers are basically the opposite of the twilighters. They consider themselves puritans of the game and are willing to sacrifice their sanity and slumber for the sake of being first on the course so they won't be held up by the less devout who think it's permissible to sleep until the sun comes up and then play a five-hour round of golf. The dew chasers tee off as the sun rises so they can finish their round by mid-morning. They then spend some time on the range or practice green, play another round, or even, in certain rare cases, use the rest of the day to have a life. Some even go home and mow the lawn.

A foursome of dew chasers found Denny's clubs littering the lot when they arrived the next morning. They followed the trail of clubs and discovered Denny behind the wheel of his car, locked in and motionless, his eyes staring straight ahead. The golfer knocked on the windshield. Denny didn't respond.

"That guy don't look right," one of them said.

"Yeah, he needs help," another added.

One of the golfers reached to open the door, then snatched his hand back. "Yech!" he exclaimed. "What the heck is this?"

"It's all over the place," his buddy said. He lifted his foot as he realized he was standing in a puddle of slime.

The sky brightened as sunrise marked the end of night. Inside the car, Denny's lip quivered, but he didn't make a sound.

Better Ball

Not every friendship forged on the golf course lasts forever. Just ask the guy in the tenth fairway staring at the six iron covered in blood. For him, the beginning of the end came when he and his buddy entered their club's better ball tournament. After that, no one lived happily ever after. In fact, one of them didn't live ever after at all.

Stuart and Arthur were more than mere friends; they were golf buddies. Both guys were average players. That is to say, they each sported a more or less accurate eighteen handicaps and played mostly for fun. Oh, they talked a lot about getting better, but never quite had the time for taking lessons and practicing on the range—the things that 'getting better' required, at least according to all the magazines. They much preferred to spend their allotted golf time on the course, where they each hit a few good shots (which they inevitably remembered) and a few clinkers (which they promptly forgot). It all kind of evened out over the span of eighteen holes. It was a particularly memorable good shot that Stuart hit, though, that changed everything and led to what happened later. Odd isn't it, that a single perfectly-struck six iron could produce so much blood?

It happened a week before the club's annual better ball tournament. Arthur had hit his tee shot safely onto the green on the par-three seventh hole. It wasn't pretty, but he was on the dance floor so he was

155

happy. Then Stuart stepped up and hit a five iron like he'd never hit one before, so smooth that he didn't even feel the club make contact. He watched the ball sail into the blue sky, crest at the top of its flight, and drop like a feather twelve inches from the hole. It hopped once and stopped on the edge of the cup.

"Damn! Nice shot!" Arthur said.

"Not bad, if I do say so myself," Stuart replied. His chest puffed out a full six inches as he became aware that now he was good. Very good. So good, in fact, that he should certainly play in the upcoming club tournament. Since he needed a partner to play in the two-man team event, he asked Arthur.

"Oh, Stuart, I don't know. Do you think we're good enough for tournament play?" Arthur answered.

"Sure we are!" Stuart exclaimed. "You've seen me play. I hit plenty of great shots!" Arthur started to protest, so Stuart added quickly, "You do, too. All we need is a little practice."

Arthur had been going to say that they also hit a lot of bad shots along with the good ones, but he didn't. Later, he would wish he had thrown several buckets of cold water on the idea. Instead, he said prophetically, "Well all right, but let's not kill ourselves over this. It's just a game, remember?"

For the remainder of the round, Stuart buckled down and played for real. He didn't hit the ball like a tour pro, but he behaved like one. He threw grass into the air to test the wind on almost every shot. He paced off the distance from the sprinkler head to his ball so he could calibrate the distance of his approach shots. He looked at every putt from three angles and putted out every hole—no gimmees in tournament play! He finished the round by beating Arthur by two strokes, 92 to 94.

Immediately after the round, Stuart signed them up for the tournament while Arthur was changing his shoes in the locker room. In the parking lot outside the clubhouse, Stuart announced, "We're going to practice every day, starting tomorrow. I'll meet you on the range after work." Arthur tried to protest that his wife wasn't going to look favorably on that, but Stuart cut him off. "We're partners in this thing, Arthur, and if you don't do your part, I swear I'll murder you." Stuart smiled when he said it, but Arthur drove home with the nasty phrase ringing in his ears.

Arthur's feeling of impending doom was reinforced the next evening when he was held up at the office and arrived at the driving range twenty minutes late. Stuart was furious. "You better get serious about this," he said between clenched teeth at the end of a ten-minute tirade on the importance of practice. Arthur didn't know what to make of that, but he didn't like the sound of it at all.

The rest of the week, each practice session was worse than the last. Arthur made it on time every other evening, but Stuart became increasingly insistent that they stay later each night, hitting more and more balls in their quest for perfection. Arthur began to believe the stories about pros who hit practice balls until their hands bled. Unfortunately, unlike the pros, the more Arthur practiced, the worse he got. Stuart didn't improve either, but he somehow only saw the good shots he hit, so his confidence just grew and grew while Arthur's shrank and shrank with every ball he sliced onto the range.

Stuart's coaching didn't help, either. It started with a couple of suggestions, but it soon became a torrent of commands. "Keep your head down," he ordered, and, "Don't let your left wrist bow at the top. Turn your left toe out a little more. Bigger shoulder turn. Don't lift your left heel." Arthur's head reeled from the onslaught.

He didn't sleep well Thursday night. Saturday was the tournament and Stuart had persuaded him to take a day off work Friday so they could play a tune-up round. As he tossed and turned, Arthur visualized Stuart's merciless glare on the range as Arthur hit clunker after clunker. Murderous rage bubbled beneath the surface as Stuart ordered him to hold his left arm straight, keep his right elbow in, plant his left heel, and on and on. "I'll murder you" resonated in his head as Arthur twitched and twisted in his bed that night.

During the practice round, Stuart was a relentless task master and, of course, Arthur couldn't do anything right. After he three-putted on the ninth green—his third three-jack of the round so far—Stuart exploded.

"You're hopeless!"

"I'm sorry, Stuart," Arthur almost sobbed.

"If you keep that up, we'll get creamed tomorrow!" Stuart ranted on.

"But I'm trying my best!" Arthur protested weakly.

"Your best isn't good enough!" Stuart snarled as he stomped off the green and into the snack bar. Arthur cringed at an imagined blow from Stuart's mallet-headed putter. He hung back while Stuart got a Coke from the snack window and headed for the tenth tee. As Arthur stepped up to the window to get a drink for himself, he saw Stuart stop to inspect the pairings for tomorrow's tournament, which were posted near the starter's shack. Stuart read down the list, then looked frantically around as if he were searching for someone. He spotted his quarry on the putting green. It was Ron Darmen, a pretty good golfer who played with Stuart and Arthur from time to time. Stuart talked with him for a minute, then the two men shook hands. Darmen got his clubs and followed Stuart to the tenth tee. Arthur paid for his Coke and walked toward the tee himself, wondering what was going on. He stopped at the starter's shack to look at the posted pairings, searching for a clue to Stuart's behavior. There was a heavy red line drawn through the name of Sammy Stanza, Darmen's partner.

"What's the deal with Stanza?" Arthur asked the grizzled starter.

"Didn't you hear? Got hit by a bus yesterday. Knocked him dead as a flounder."

"Gee, that's a shame," Arthur said. "What's Darmen going to do about a partner?" He was immediately shocked at his own callous focus on the golf tournament instead of on the sad passing of a man's life. I'm turning into Stuart, he thought with alarm.

"Unless somebody else's partner shows up dead, Darmen's out," the starter said. Arthur turned and stared at the tenth tee, where Stuart and Ron Darmen were laughing and carrying on like fraternity brothers at their ten-year reunion. Arthur's head felt disconnected from his body as he stumbled slowly toward them. He saw it all, now: Stuart intended to get a new partner. Unreality gripped Arthur's overwrought and sleep-deprived brain. Stuart said something to him as he walked onto the tee, but Arthur just stared at him blankly.

"Earth to Arthur!" Stuart repeated. "Ron is going to play the back nine with us. Okay?" Darmen stepped up and stuck out his hand. Arthur shook it absently. The human contact brought him back to the real world, at least for a moment.

"Oh...uh...sure," he mumbled. He thought Stuart and Darmen exchanged knowing glances and his fear started to mount.

Stuart teed off first, hitting a weak fade that landed on the edge of the fairway. Ron Darmen insisted on hitting last, so Arthur teed his ball up and tried to calm himself. His practice swing dug a six-inch furrow in the grass and Stuart groaned. Arthur glanced at his partner nervously, shook the dirt off his driver, and managed to hit a big banana slice into the trees. Then Darmen stepped up and nailed a screamer right down the middle of the fairway.

"Yo! Killer!" Stuart exclaimed with a huge grin on his face.

Arthur knew his fate was sealed. A pink haze glowed in front of his eyes as he trudged toward the trees to hunt for his ball. Stuart chuckled at something Darmen said as the two of them strode down the fairway, almost arm-in-arm. "Where are they going to do it?" Arthur said to himself. He visualized the holes ahead, stopping mentally at the fifteenth. It was perfect. Far from the clubhouse, the green was surrounded by woods. It was the ideal place to leave a body!

His hands trembled as he chopped at his ball among the tree roots. By the time he managed to hack his way out, Stuart and Ron Darmen were down the fairway. Arthur thought about running back to the safety of the clubhouse, but Stuart motioned for him to hurry up, so he grabbed a six iron from his bag and slashed a hurried shot from the rough.

Maybe it was fear-induced adrenaline or perhaps it was some horrific subconscious force at work, but Arthur's club ripped through the long grass and the ball streaked through the air like a surface-to-air missile. Arthur saw Stuart and Darmen chatting amiably ahead. The world went into slow motion as Arthur watched the ball hurtle directly toward them. Arthur tried to yell "fore!" but it was as if he were caught in one of those nightmares where he screamed but no sound came out. The fatal rocket smashed into Stuart's head. He crumpled to the ground.

Arthur stood speechless for a moment, then ran toward the fairway. Or at least, he tried to run but it was as if he were swimming in molasses. Captive in his nightmare, Arthur struggled up the fairway until finally he stood over Stuart's body. Darmen knelt beside Stuart trying to find a pulse. A thin line of blood trickled from Stuart's hairline where Arthur's ball had cracked his skull.

"My God, I think he's dead," Darmen said, his eyes wide.

Arthur didn't reply. What could he say? He discovered that he was still holding his six-iron in his hand and used it to gently prod Stuart's thigh. When Stuart didn't respond, a wave of horror washed over Arthur, followed by one of relief. The world started to come back into focus. No Stuart, he thought, means no tournament. He sucked in air as if he had been holding his breath for a week, which, in essence, he had been.

Darmen broke through Arthur's fog with a polite cough. "Maybe this isn't the best time," he said, "But would you want to play with me in the tournament tomorrow? I mean, since we both need partners and everything." With a hopeful smile, he offered his hand to Arthur to seal the partnership.

The air turned crimson and every muscle in Arthur's body snapped into one big, hard knot. The brutal hours on the practice range with Stuart, the verbal abuse and bullying, the non-stop derisive remarks about Arthur's swing all came back to him. Why couldn't they understand? He didn't want to compete, he just wanted to play the game! He wanted to get better, sure, but not so he could beat somebody else on the course. Arthur wanted nothing more than a simple round of golf. Hit the ball, find it, hit it again. Smell some roses along the way and tilt your head back on the green to enjoy the sunshine on your face every once in a while. That's what the game was all about!

He looked past the kneeling Darmen at Stuart lying in a puddle of blood. "He ruined it for me," Arthur said.

"What do you mean?" Darmen asked.

"Golf. He ruined golf. And now you're doing the same."

Darmen's smile disappeared as Arthur wound up for another swing.

Balderwhipple

Minerva teed up her ball just ever so. First, she stood where she would stand to take her actual swing so she could make sure it was a perfectly level area and that no stray tufts of grass or debris would be behind her ball to distract her on her takeaway. Then she very carefully pushed the tee into the ground, keeping it perfectly vertical and adjusting its height so that exactly half of the ball showed above the top of her driver. She steadied the ball on the tee and turned it so that the logo was pointed in the direction she wanted the ball to go. Finally, she checked, twice, to be sure she had not teed her ball ahead of the markers, which would have meant a penalty stroke.

When Minerva was finished teeing her ball, she stepped away from it to perform the same pre-shot routine she went through on every shot. First, she stood several paces behind the ball, looking for the line of flight she desired it to follow. She chose a mark on the ground eighteen inches ahead of the ball on that line. Then she stepped to her ball and put the club down facing the target, stepping first with her right foot and then with her left, taking up the perfect position so that her body was aligned correctly. She double-checked her grip, double-checked her stance, turned her head and looked once to visualize where the ball was supposed to land on the fairway. Then, she closed her eyes.

Minerva took a deep breath, exhaled half of it, and said, quite audibly but to herself, "Balderwhipple!" She opened her eyes, drew the club back smoothly, paused at the top of her backswing in perfect form, and drove the ball right down the middle of the fairway one hundred and fifty-five yards, leaving herself another one hundred and fifty-five yards to the green.

By the time her ball landed in the fairway, the men in the foursome on the back tee were hopping from one leg to the other and pounding their drivers into the ground in frustration.

Balderwhipple?

Susan, the new girl in the foursome, wondered what that little phrase was all about, but, being new to the game and not wanting to seem completely ignorant, she tucked the question away to be asked at a more opportune time. Besides, the men fuming on the tee behind her made her nervous. She noticed that the men didn't seem to bother Minerva or the other two women in her group, though. One of them, Alice, exchanged glances with the other, Eugenia, who raised her left eyebrow a millimeter, but, other than that, their expressions never changed as Minerva smiled shyly and stepped away from the tee so her playing partners could take their turns.

"Nice shot, dear," Alice said.

"Very nice indeed," Eugenia said. "But you weren't supposed to get a stroke on this hole. You should hit again without the . . . you know." She looked at Susan out of the corner of her eye. Susan was puzzling over the reference to a stroke, since she thought that a stroke like that had something to do with the handicap system that you took care of on the scorecard. Besides, she was horrified at the thought of holding up the men any longer. Take another shot? They would be furious! Susan sighed in relief when Eugenia added, "But never mind. We'll give you one this time."

Alice and Eugenia took a little less time on the tee than Minerva, but still didn't hurry. Their drives were mirror images of each other, one landing in the left rough, the other in the right, both slightly shorter than Minerva's.

Now it was Susan's turn. Susan had just recently started playing golf at her husband's insistence. They were new in town and he felt joining the country club and taking up the game would help her make some new friends. He had arranged for lessons and taken her out to play a couple of times himself, but this was the first time Susan had played with anyone else. Her palms were perspiring.

"Don't be nervous, dear," Minerva said, which, of course, made Susan even shakier. Every tidbit of instruction she had ever received flashed into her head as she stepped up to the tee. Alignment, grip, head steady, balance, turn, weight shift, extend, contract, firm, loose; it all flooded through her brain and right down to her knees, which started quaking. All of the feeling left her hands as she pulled her driver back limply and she may have even closed her eyes—she wasn't sure—as the club head raced past the ball, missing it by several inches. She thought she heard one of the men say, "Oh for godsakes, lady."

"That's perfectly all right! We've all done it, haven't we girls?" Minerva said, nodding encouragingly at Alice and Eugenia, who smiled back helpfully.

"Just take your time and do it again," Alice said.

"Keep your eyes open this time!" one of the men yelled. Susan tee-tered for a moment on the edge between mortified hysteria and murder-ous anger at the ranting men behind her, but got control of herself and re-addressed the ball with a determined look.

"That's a girl," Minerva said. As Susan reached the top of her back-swing, a crow flapped down to land on the tee just at the edge of her vision. It distracted her for just a moment, but she snapped her eyes back to the waiting ball and smacked it as hard as she could. The ball skidded along the grass but stopped in the center of the fairway a respectable hundred yards from the tee. The crow cawed triumphantly. "See, that wasn't so bad, was it?" Minerva said as they climbed into their cart.

"Let's keep it moving today, ladies!" one of the men called as they drove away.

"Awk!" answered the crow, which flew ahead of the carts up the fairway.

Susan hacked her way through the rest of the first hole, trying to play as fast as she could. Even though Alice, Eugenia, and Minerva didn't hurry, they didn't play much better than Susan did, although Alice sank a very long putt that left everyone feeling better as they walked off the green.

* * *

"Now, you do get a stroke on this hole, Minerva," Eugenia said af-ter she and Alice had teed off on the second hole. It was a par five, not particularly long, but with a creek that ran along the right side and crossed the fairway in front of the green.

"Oh, good!" Minerva chirped. The crow, which had been pecking around on the ground near their carts, walked up onto the tee as if to watch. Minerva went through her meticulous setup, addressed the ball, took a deep breath, and said "Balderwhipple" just before she drew back her club to swing. Her drive sailed straight and true down the middle of the fairway and bounced down nearly two hundred yards away.

"Awk!" went the crow.

"Oh wow!" said Susan.

Minerva looked very, very pleased. "It's your turn, dear," she said to Susan. Susan teed up her ball and tried to concentrate, but the men behind them were walking off the first green. She rushed her swing, trying to hit before they got to the tee, and knocked her shot into the creek off on the right.

"No do-overs, ladies!" one of the men called as if reading Susan's mind. He was a big man with an intimidating swagger made bigger by his paunch. He stood on the back tee while his companions clambered out of their carts. One of them, a swarthy fellow wearing a wide-brimmed plantation hat, added, "Let's try to finish the round while it's daylight, okay?" Susan wanted to crawl into her golf bag and hide.

"Come along, girls," Eugenia said. "We'll deal with them later." She and Alice got into their cart and took off. As Susan sat down in the cart with Minerva, the crow flapped away and landed near the water where Susan's ball had disappeared. His flight distracted Susan from the men long enough for her to remember that some strange things were going on. She was about to ask what "Balderwhipple" meant when Minerva pulled the cart up next to the creek.

"Good job, Elroy," Minerva said. Susan's heart missed a beat as the crow dropped her dripping ball onto a patch of short grass in front of the cart.

"Awk!" it said and hopped out of the way. Susan turned to Minerva with wide eyes and a slack jaw.

"It's all right, dear," Minerva said soothingly. "We're going to give you a stroke on every hole from now on." Susan started to ask what that meant, but Minerva preempted her question. "But you should hit your ball now. I think the barbarians are getting restless." Susan came back to the present as she heard the men shouting something unpleasant from the tee. She jumped out of the cart and snatched a club out of her bag. "Just relax and swing slowly," Minerva smiled.

As Susan stood over her ball trying to collect herself, Minerva discretely raised her right hand and extended the first two fingers toward her. When Susan pulled back her club, Minerva's fingers followed the club head into the air, then described a small, quick arc downward that Susan's swing seemed to mimic. The ball jumped off of the clubface and rocketed down the fairway, landing next to Minerva's. Susan stood, dumbfounded, until Minerva said, "See? Just swing slowly."

"Now hurry up and hit it again!" the swaggering man with the paunch shouted from the tee. Susan jumped back into the cart but Minerva deliberately gave the man a long, threatening look over her shoulder before she turned the cart up the fairway. The crow flew lazily above them, out of Susan's sight. Between her exultation at the superb shot and her acute awareness of the nasty men behind them, Susan forgot to ask Minerva about the crow and the other strange things that were happening.

Susan and Minerva hit their next shots and were just driving away toward the green when they heard the crack of a club. A ball sailed past their cart on the right and rolled to a stop near the rough. "Fore" someone behind them yelled after the ball stopped rolling. That was followed by ragged laughter. Susan's dread of looking foolish morphed temporarily into defiance. "Drive back," she snapped. "I'm going to give those ugly men a taste of what-for!"

Surprisingly, Minerva remained calm. "Not now, dear," she cooed. "I have something else in mind." Susan sputtered in frustration but her normal timidity took over and she looked fearfully back at the men. The roller-coaster ride of emotions was beginning to tire her. Just then, the crow flew over the man's ball and dropped a load of white crap on it. "That's not what I'm thinking of," Minerva added, "although I second the motion."

Susan worked up the nerve to ask hesitantly, "Minerva, what's going on here?"

"Nothing to be concerned about right now, Susan," Minerva replied. "I know you have some questions, but I'll answer them later." An enigmatic smile played across her face. "Let's just concentrate on our game for now, shall we?" For some reason, Susan felt reassured. Golf was turning out to be a more exciting game than she had envisioned. Deep down inside, hidden under layers of shyness and self-doubt, Susan kind of liked it.

* * *

By the time the women had finished their putts on the second hole, the men were stomping around in the fairway waiting to hit their shots onto the green. Their language was filthy and obviously meant to be overheard. As they walked off the green, Alice and Eugenia glared angrily back down the fairway. Minerva's visage was unnaturally calm, though, almost beneficent. "I think we should let the boys play through on the next hole, don't you girls?" she said. Alice and Eugenia smiled grimly at each other and nodded. They drove their carts to the back tee on the third hole, a par three with a generous green protected by sand traps on either side and a pond in front. Alice and Eugenia got out of their cart and rummaged around in their golf bags while they waited for the men to finish putting on the green they had just left. Alice drew a club with a black shaft and oddly angled silver head out of her bag, while Eugenia took a black towel with silver markings on it out of hers.

"It won't be long now, dear," Minerva said as she stepped out and went around to her own bag, where she dug into a pocket and found a black glove with silver markings like those on Eugenia's towel. The crow settled onto the roof of the cart above her head, adding to Susan's sudden sense of dread. She wasn't sure which frightened her more, the brutish men or the three decidedly threatening women in her foursome with their winged black companion. The men drove raucously up the hill to the tee and Susan got out of her cart.

"Why don't you fellows play through?" Minerva said with an ingratiating smile. "I think we must be holding you up today."

The swarthy man with the wide-brimmed hat muttered, "You can say that again," as he got heavily out of his cart.

"Oh no, not at all," said the swaggering man with the paunch. The other two men simply smirked. One of them lit a cigar and hitched up his shorts. He stepped onto the tee and ostentatiously paced off the distance from today's tee markers to the official yardage plaque.

"One seventy three, boys," he announced.

"Let's get at it. We don't want to hold up these ladies," the fourth man said as he teed up his ball. Then he looked in Susan's direction and winked. Eugenia raised the black towel to her face as if to wipe away some perspiration and muttered something into it. She held the towel over her eyes as the man swung and whiffed the ball just like Susan had done on the first tee. A moment of stunned silence passed, then his partners started guffawing and hooting. The man glared at them and swung again. This time he hit the ball a glancing blow and it plopped weakly into the trap on the right side of the green.

"That's two!" the swaggering man chortled.

"Awk!" went the crow.

The man in the Bermuda shorts laid his cigar carefully on top of the tee marker and prepared to swing as his partner stormed off the tee. Alice casually pointed her black-shafted club at the cigar and traced a small figure eight in the air with the oddly-angled silver head. The cigar started to vibrate as the man went into his backswing. Just as he swung down, it jumped into the air and exploded into a shower of sparks. The man's ball whistled into the pond.

"You bastards!" he shouted, dropping his club and slapping madly at the sparks burning on his shirt. Susan shrank back in fear, thinking he was cursing at them, but when he demanded, "Who loaded that cigar!" she realized he thought his buddies had pulled a practical joke on him. The other men stopped laughing to see which one of them was going to take credit for the gag, but, when no one stepped forward, a confused silence fell on them.

"Awk!" observed the crow.

"Oh my," exclaimed Minerva. Alice and Eugenia smiled vacantly while Susan stood in silence. The man who had hit his ball into the sand trap looked suspiciously at the women as he stepped away from the tee.

The swarthy man took a vicious practice swing, teed up his ball, then slashed the air with his club again. Minerva's black-gloved fingers wiggled down by her side and her thumb pointed at the man's broad-brimmed plantation hat. Just as he swung, the hat blew off and landed on his ball. His club slashed through it, made contact with the ball, and sent both ball and hat dribbling five yards ahead to the front tee.

"Awk!" went the crow again.

There was a moment of stunned silence, then Minerva asked no one in particular, "Does that mean he has to play his next shot from the ladies' tee?"

"Shut up, lady!" snapped the man whose hat lay crushed over his ball on the front tee. He turned to his cohorts and stated officiously, "That doesn't count. Interference." This set off a furious argument. While they were cursing at each other, Minerva motioned for Alice and Eugenia to come closer.

"You do the next one," she whispered in Susan's ear.

Susan hesitated for a moment while she thought about the consequences of her decision. "But I don't know how," she whispered back, still uncertain.

"This will help," Alice answered as she gave her the black-shafted club with the oddly angled silver head.

"Here, take this," Eugenia added, draping the black towel around her shoulders.

Minerva whispered, "Just take my hand and concentrate on the man while he swings." She held out her black-gloved hand and Susan took it. Alice took Minerva's other hand and Eugenia gripped Alice's, completing the chain. Their strength flowed into Susan and she didn't even flinch when Elroy settled onto her shoulder and snuggled against her cheek.

"You'll all play them as they lie!" snarled the man with the paunch as he swaggered up to the tee. "Now shut up and let me show you how a real man plays this game." His partners muttered but went silent. The man looked over at the women after he teed up his ball. "Just watch this, ladies," he smirked. None of the girls said anything, but Susan stared directly into his eyes so hard he recoiled slightly. Then he blinked and took a huge practice swing.

Susan concentrated just as hard as she could on the man's stance, his alignment, his grip, his posture. She visualized the flight of his ball. She gripped Minerva's black-gloved hand and felt a pleasant electric tingle run up her arm, through her chest, and into her heart. As the man drew back the club ever so deliberately, Susan's eyes narrowed and she fixed her stare on his ball. He paused at the top, then swung powerfully through the ball, making perfect contact. Susan's unblinking eyes followed the ball into the air, over the pond, and onto the green, where it bounced once before it rolled into the hole.

"Hole in one!" the man screamed. His arms flew up and he danced around the tee in triumph while the other men jumped up and down hooting and hollering. "That's how a real man does it!" he shouted.

He looked at Susan, who locked her eyes on his, then snapped her head back toward the hole. His eyes followed just in time to see his ball spring straight up out of the hole, bounce twice impossibly on the very tip of the flag stick, then float slowly back through the air toward them until it was directly over the pond. It hovered a moment before dropping into the pond with a feeble splash.

173

"Awk!" went the crow on Susan's shoulder.

The man turned back to Susan with a look of disbelief that changed to horror. She batted her eyelashes at him and said with a sly smile, "Let's keep up the pace of play, shall we?"

Bald Peter's Pond

The boy looked innocent enough fooling around in the shallow water at the edge of Bald Peter's Pond, but Stanley knew he was just a lawsuit waiting to happen. He couldn't have been more than ten years old, maybe eight. From the look of his clothes, he probably came from the housing project on the other side of the expressway not far from the course. Regardless, he had parents. And parents could sue. Stanley knew about lawsuits like those. That's how he made his rather excellent living.

The boy was probably looking for lost balls, but he was wading in and out of the water less than two hundred yards from the tee where Stanley stood—just about where a slicer's ball would come hurtling down. Stanley was surprised that the club let the boy play around on the course, and even more shocked when George Bisterman teed off without so much as a single "Fore!" Even though the drive landed safely in the fairway, it wasn't smart. A personal injury lawyer, Stanley knew how vulnerable George would be to a lawsuit by the boy's parents. The club, too, for that matter, since it had obviously done nothing to keep him out of harm's way. The idea of giving the boy his business card crossed Stanley's mind, but, in a rare twinge of conscience, he dismissed it as a poor way to return George's invitation to play at the club. He might be what some people called an "ambulance chaser," but Stanley wasn't a complete boor.

He had just decided to say something about the potential liability to George when a ball plopped into the pond from the fifteenth tee on the other side of the pond and the boy disappeared. He didn't dive under the water—he just suddenly wasn't there. Stanley frowned in disbelief and stared hard at the pond where the boy had been standing waist deep in the murky water. There wasn't a single ripple on the surface to indicate that anyone had been there just a moment ago. He looked over toward the other side of the pond, expecting to see the boy surfacing there, ball in hand, but all he saw was a disgusted golfer walking toward the water from the fifteenth fairway, obviously looking for his ball. Just then, Stanley was distracted by the crack of a driver against a ball as another player in his group teed off, again oblivious to the boy who was somewhere out there in harm's way.

Bald Peter's Pond separates the fourteenth and fifteenth holes at Blasted Stick Golf Club. Slicers like Stanley hate it because the fourteenth is a long hole that curves to the right around the pond so that both your tee shot and your approach shot have the water in play. The fifteenth hole is no better. It's a sharp dog-leg left that comes back along the other side of the pond, bending away from it only at the crook in the dog leg. Unless you can draw your tee shot perfectly away from the water, it's best to lay up with a mid-iron because anything hit to the right is automatically wet and anything shot too long can carry through the fairway and end up in the pond as well. That's why the members often call it "Ball Eater's Pond" as well as its traditional name.

Stanley could tell he would grow to hate Bald Peter's Pond if he were a member. He was playing the course for the first time at the invitation of George, for whom Stanley had won a six-figure settlement in a lawsuit over a can of dog food that supposedly gave George's faithful Rottweiler a tummy ache. The potential for more business with George aside, Stanley didn't think he wanted to belong to Blasted Stick. Play was slow and irksome, giving him extra time to contemplate the many bad things that could go wrong with his swing. That was especially true on the fourteenth tee where Stanley stood with an unimpeded view of the balls flying into the water from the fifteenth hole as well as his own. There were so many balls dimpling the water it looked like the pond was in a hail storm. It was very unnerving.

Stanley's caddie handed him his driver and stated the obvious: stay left. Stanley teed up a brand-new Breakstone D4, the latest in high-priced golf ball technology. As he addressed the ball, he tried to visualize anything except his shot slicing out over the water. But it was like the old schoolboy bet that, try as hard as you might, you can't not think of an elephant. He looked down the fairway before he started his back-swing and glimpsed a head ducking beneath the surface of the water. He swung anyway. His ball splashed down in the exact spot where he had seen the boy. George groaned in sympathy.

As they walked off the tee, Stanley's caddie said, "You may be okay. The boy's there."

"What do you mean?" Stanley asked. "I saw the ball splash in the pond."

"Maybe, maybe not," the caddie answered.

Stanley looked at him closely. What did the boy have to do with anything. Or maybe the caddie was offering to cheat! Was he planning to surreptitiously drop another ball in the rough? Stanley didn't have many scruples, but they couldn't get away with that. "You don't have a hole in your pocket, do you?" Stanley asked. The last thing Stanley wanted was for the caddie to drop a ball down his pant leg and pretend to find it. Everyone on the tee saw the ball go into the water.

"No sir! But the boy may have found your ball and tossed it up on the bank. You can play it without penalty—local rule."

"That can't be right," Stanley said as they walked along in the rough.

"Sure it is," the caddie answered. "It's an interpretation of rule 19, outside agency. In this case, since the boy is what he is, you play it like you find it."

"What do you mean, 'what he is'?"

Now it was the caddie's turn to give Stanley a look of surprise. "I thought you knew that, sir. The boy's a ghost. Dead as Hamlet's father. Bald Peter was the first greenskeeper here at Blasted Stick. He caught the boy fishing up balls and selling them to the members. Bald Peter wanted to sell those balls himself, so the story goes, so he kept chasing the boy off the course. Then one day a couple of members found the boy floating face down in the pond. That's the story, anyways. Nobody ever proved anything but that's how the pond came by its name.

"Wait a minute!" Stanley exclaimed. "Are you trying to tell me there's a ghost in the pond that retrieves lost balls?"

"Yes sir. Not every ball, though. Only the ones he can find."

"That's preposterous!" Stanley scoffed. He started to say something else, but the words froze in his mouth when the caddie pointed down at a ball lying in the tall grass at their feet. It was Stanley's Breakstone D4 and it was five feet away from the pond. Stanley looked up at the caddie, who shrugged and nodded. Stanley looked past him to the pond, but the sunlight glinted off the surface so that he couldn't see anything. While he was watching, another ball from the fifteenth hole plopped into the water on the other side.

"The only thing is, you gotta pay the boy for the ball," the caddie said. "Most guys put a dollar on the ground. Some leave more."

Now Stanley understood what was going on. The caddies had a little scam going! They would con some unsuspecting guest into leaving money on the ground, then a caddie from the following group would pick it up. The members probably were in on it as a prank. Very funny. Well, Stanley wasn't a member of the bar association because he was stupid. He'd seen a scam or two in his time.

"Sure," he said with a big wink at the caddie. "Will this do?" He tossed a twenty dollar bill on the ground. The caddie gasped but didn't say anything while Stanley took a seven wood out of the bag. Stanley hit a decent shot out of the wet grass while the caddie stared open-mouthed at the money on the ground. Stanley handed him the club, then reached down and snatched the twenty off the grass.

"I'm not stupid you know," he growled. "It only took my three tries to pass the bar exam."

"But . . . but you shouldn't tease him like that," the astounded caddie protested.

"Oh yeah? Watch me." Stanley stuffed the bill into his pocket and strode away congratulating himself on scamming the scammers. He heard a small splash in the pond behind him and whirled to see if the group on the tee was hitting into them, but they were just standing and waiting, talking among themselves. He shrugged off an uneasy feeling and headed for the green, his silent caddie trailing behind.

No one else in the group said anything on the green, although Stanley thought he saw George and the other two members exchange knowing glances with the caddies. He chuckled to himself and waited until they were walking to the fifteenth tee to mention the incident to George.

"Do a lot of guests fall for the dead boy in the pond routine?" he smirked.

"What routine?" George asked.

"You know, the scam where the caddie drops a ball and says it was tossed out of the water by the dead boy in the pond?" Stanley said with a knowing chuckle.

"Oh that!" George said. "That's just kind of a superstition. We all do it. Leave a dollar for the boy, I mean. It's harmless and kind of fun." He turned to Stanley's caddie as they got to the fifteenth tee. "Did you tell Stanley the story of the boy who drowned in Bald Peter's Pond?"

"Yes sir." The caddie looked down at the clubs and away from Stanley's smirk. "But he didn't leave anything for the boy," he mumbled as if he were ashamed.

"So what happens?" Stanley asked. "Do I get a penalty stroke?" The other guys laughed nervously as George half-jokingly said that wouldn't be necessary. Stanley laughed along with them, but the caddies didn't and Stanley thought they had all grown a little sullen. If that attitude didn't change by the end of the round, he thought, someone's going to get a pretty small tip.

The three members were all hitting irons off of the fifteenth tee, playing it safely to the dog leg and avoiding the water. "What do you think?" Stanley asked his caddie, "Four iron or five?" The caddie asked

Stanley almost insolently if he could hit a draw. It sounded like a challenge to Stanley, which sealed the fate of the man's tip. Stanley's male hormones took over as he said, "Of course I can hit a draw. Give me a three iron." If he hit a perfect high draw, he would be in superb shape for a birdie. Unfortunately, Stanley had never hit a perfect high draw in his life and he didn't even come close to hitting one now. His ball sailed out in its usual parabola to the right and splashed into the pond.

"Pushing your luck with the boy in the pond, aren't you?" George chuckled. Stanley glared at his caddie and stalked down the fairway with George's comment ringing in his ears.

Stanley approached the edge of the pond but his caddie seemed to be hanging back. "No monkey business with another ball down your pants leg," Stanley hissed sternly over his shoulder. As he edged closer to the water, he could see a ball lying just within reach in the shallow water. There was some moss floating around on the surface, though, so he could not quite make out the logo. "I think that's it," he said to the caddie. "See if you can reach it." The caddie made no move toward the water and actually stammered a warning as he backed away from the water's edge. "Give me a club," Stanley snapped. When the caddie didn't respond, Stanley yanked the sand wedge out of his bag.

"Don't get so close to the water!" the caddie pleaded.

Stanley snorted derisively and slid carefully down the shallow bank. His spikes held fast and he reached toward the ball with his wedge. The moss floated around the club head and the ball seemed to move away from him. It was just a little bit further out that he thought, so he bent and stretched forward, teetering on the very edge. His foot slipped slightly. "Give me a hand here," he ordered, reaching back toward the caddie. The man ignored Stanley's outstretched hand.

The caddie stood frozen in place. He stared wide-eyed at the pond. He tried to say something, but his mouth just flapped open and shut.

Suddenly, something yanked the sand wedge and pulled Stanley past the tipping point. He splashed face-down into the pond. His feet kicked helplessly on the bank as his head and shoulders slide into the gooshy muck on the bottom of the pond.

"Help!" the caddie yelled. George ran over and grabbed one leg while the other caddie clamped onto the other but they couldn't haul the beefy lawyer out of the pond. It was as if something under the water had a death grip on him and was pulling him deeper. Two of the other players grabbed Stanley's belt. The four men pulled as hard as they could while Stanley bucked frantically to get his face out of the muck, but something beneath the surface pulled harder.

Stanley's struggles weakened and finally ceased entirely. When he went limp in their hands, Stanley's caddy jumped into the pond and grabbed his shirt.

"All together—heave!" he shouted.

With a slurping gurgle like a giant suction cup releasing, Stanley's head came up out of the mud. The men dragged him onto the bank. Someone dashed to the clubhouse for help while the caddie rolled Stanley over onto his back. He pinched Stanley's muddy nose and pried open his flaccid lips to start mouth-to-mouth resuscitation. He shoved his fingers into Stanley's mouth to push the tongue out of the way, then recoiled in horror as the lawyer gagged.

"Sit him up!" George cried.

The caddie grabbed Stanley's arms and heaved him upright. Stanley's eyes popped open. Thick black mud gushed from his mouth. He choked and coughed, his throat straining as he tried to force something up from his gullet. With a great explosion of muck, the object flew from his lips and plopped on the ground between his legs. It was a brand new Breakstone D4.

Three Club Wind

You don't need fourteen clubs to play golf. You need three. I know you don't believe me, but you'll play better if you aren't distracted by those eleven other superfluous implements.

Why don't you need a bag full of clubs? Because you hit most of them the same distance anyway: 147 yards. I know, I checked.

Oh, I know once you hit a five iron 160 yards that you were sure would have rolled out to 175 if only that bunker hadn't been in the way. And yes, you have been known to hit a driver 193 yards (that looked like 240), but that's 147 yards straight and 46 yards sideways, so it doesn't change the math. Nor does the power of positive thinking change the distance. You don't hit it 280 or even 240. That only happens in your wet dreams, so get over it.

Seriously, you hit all your clubs 147 yards. Go to the range and check it out. Hit ten balls each with all the clubs except your putter and measure—accurately—the ones that land ten yards either side of where you were aiming. Some will go a tiny bit farther, many will go less, but between skulls, chunks, banana balls, and maybe three accidentally perfect swings, the average will be 147 yards. Less for wedges, which I'll get to in a minute.

So you might as well get rid of all the long clubs in your bag except one. I suggest a five iron since you hit it 160 that one time. And yes,

185

chuck the driver. Turn it into a lamp or something useful. You can't hit the side of a barn from the inside with it anyway. Maybe you can use it in your garden as a $400 stake for your tomato plants.

Now pick a wedge—any wedge. You hit them all pretty much the same distance, too, although it varies on any given shot depending on whether you chunk it or skull it. But you can do that with any wedge, so why do you need four of them? Sand? You can't get it out in less than two strokes with anything, so don't bother. Lob? Go ahead, Phil, make my day. One wedge is all you need.

And, of course, you need a putter. When you play with three clubs, the key to scoring is putting well. But isn't that always the case?

Actually, considering the way you putt, you'd probably do just as well with the five iron. I know a guy who putted with a seven iron, but he was a little strange in other ways, too. No, it's okay. Carry a putter. We don't want to mess with tradition too much.

Five iron, wedge, putter. You think I'm kidding about playing with three clubs but I'm not. I've done it plenty of times and scored just as well as when I hauled around fourteen clubs—and done it faster.

The speed comes mostly from not spending any time figuring out to the millimeter exactly how far you are from the pin so you can choose exactly the right club. Are you 195 or 198 yards? A hybrid or a soft five wood? Check the sprinkler head, pace it off. Double check with your GPS gizmo. Wait a minute and check it again after the satellite moves a quarter degree across the sky. What's your buddy's GPS say? It's a different brand, so it will naturally read 187 or 204. Too bad you don't have a laser range finder, too, then you could check it digitally three ways. Don't forget it's uphill, so add another five yards. But you're playing downwind, so subtract three. Oh yeah, you better take one club less because your adrenaline is flowing—there's fifty cents riding on this hole!

As if any of this matters. No matter what club you hit it with, the ball is only going to travel 147 yards, so go ahead and use your five iron. You'll save ten minutes of angst-ridden mathematics and you won't have to play your third shot out of those nasty bunkers in front of the green.

And don't even think about pacing off the distance for your wedge shot. You don't know how far you're going to hit it anyway, so what difference does it make? Seriously, here's a tip for any shot under a hundred yards: imagine how hard you'd have to throw the ball underhanded to hit it to the hole. That's how hard to swing your wedge.

Come to think of it, that's something you can do on the green when you're putting. Saves a lot of time. We could talk about reading putts, too, but that would take all day.

Still think three clubs aren't enough? Do the math. Let's assume, like most morons, you're playing from the tips and the course measures 7,000 yards. If you're playing from tees that measure anything longer, you're hopeless anyway. You should be playing from 6,200 yards and you'd have a lot more fun if you did, but that's the subject of another rant.

That 7,000-yard course has 18 holes that average 389 yards. If you hit your five iron twice, that puts you within a hundred yards (147 times 2 equals 294). Wedge it on, make a putt and you've got a par. Two-putt like usual, and you've got a bogey—still better than you'd normally score after slicing a driver into the woods, chipping out to the rough, chunking it into the bunker, skulling it out of the bunker and over the green, dribbling it on with a lob wedge out of the rough behind the green, and two-putting for a seven. But gee, you got to use six different clubs!

Not all holes will play the average distance, of course. What about that 440 yard par four? Again, do the arithmetic. Take off your socks and count on your toes if you have to. Three 147-yard five irons put you in the middle of the green, Einstein. Or a 550-yard par five? Three fives and a wedge. What, you were going to get there in two with a driver and a three wood? Who are you kidding?

But wait a minute, what about the par threes? Unless there's one over 294 yards (147 times two), you can get to every one of them in two strokes. Most of the time, you're going to need a five iron and a half-wedge, which can be a little uncomfortable. So why not hit two full wedges? There's no rule against it and it looks the same on the score-card.

Water in front? Lay up, genius.

Yeah, yeah, I know you won't have many (any?) birdie putts this way, but how many did you really have in your last round? No—real birdie putts. Ninety feet away on the apron doesn't count. Embarrassing, isn't it? Let's face it, most of the time you're putting for bogey anyway.

Actually, if you played from the right set of tees (6,200 yards or less), you'd probably be able to reach about a third of the holes in regulation with some combination of your trusty five iron and wedge, which brings six birdies into the realm of the possible—five more than you have in most rounds, right?

I will grant that playing with three clubs can get boring. The short grass in the fairway all looks the same, whereas the cart paths, fescue, and forests where you usually play add a lot of variety to your golf experience. And you'll miss the adrenaline rush that comes from bombing one over the pond on the sixth hole like you did that one time three years ago.

Besides, what are you going to do with the hour you save every round by not doing all those calculations to choose the right club? My suggestion: practice your putting.

Ben Hogan's Secret

Henry Harrington's head hurt. In fact, it was killing him. He felt like someone had peeled back the top of his skull with a dull axe, poured boiling oil into the brain pan, then nailed it shut with steel spikes. As he walked through the parking lot toward the clubhouse, his vision blurred, cleared, wavered, and cleared again. He should just turn around and go home, he thought, but he forced himself to keep walking. The club championship started tomorrow and he desperately need to fix his swing before he took on that upstart Willie Littlebart in the first match.

Henry hurried into the locker room. He waved vaguely to Pepe, the attendant, but Pepe didn't wave back. Henry didn't care. He was late. He made a beeline for his locker and kicked off his shoes. As he bent to tie his golf shoes, he felt like the top of his head was going to fall off. Maybe I ought to go see a doctor, he thought, but stood up and went for the aspirin bottle Pepe kept on his counter instead.

Photos of golf's greats lined the walls of the locker room, most taken during the Golden State Open, a near-major tournament played at the course in the heyday of the game. Byron Nelson, Sam Snead, Lloyd Mangrum, Jackie Burke, and other giants of the links looked down from the walls. They were all long dead now, but their legends lived on. Henry's idol, Ben Hogan, stared impassively from a photo next to the door leading out to the first tee. Hogan had won the Golden State twice dur-

191

ing his career, once before his terrible automobile accident and once after. His second victory came the final time the tournament was played at the club.

Pepe was noisily running shoes under the buffing wheel, so Henry helped himself to four aspirin, waved thanks as he washed them down, and slipped out the door. As he did superstitiously before every round, Henry nodded and said, "Mr. Hogan" as he tipped an imaginary hat in homage to the man as he passed his portrait.

Henry rushed down the path to the range, intent on salvaging what time he could with Rocky Pizarro, the club pro. Traffic had been a killer and then there had been that ugly incident in the parking lot, too. Henry wanted to go back and give that guy a piece of his mind, but he didn't have time now.

He hoped Rocky would still have a time slot for him. He'd talked the pro into squeezing him into his schedule because he really needed a lesson before the match. Willie Littlebart was going to be tough. He was young, flat-bellied, fearless, and hungry for his first win. Henry was a grizzled veteran, having won the championship three years before, but his belly was far from flat and he knew his days were numbered. He thought he had one more championship in him, though, if he could just get rid of the nasty hook he'd developed during the last month. He was counting on Rocky to spot the cause and give him a quick fix.

As he passed the first tee, Henry was distracted by the sight of a five-some walking down the fairway. Since when was that allowed? Golden State Country Club was a very traditional golf club, certainly not a place where five players were allowed to clog up the course. Yet there were Jim Mullien, Brad Dickens, Ernie Westerhouse, Wally Einhorn, and Brian Houston strolling along like they had all the time in the world. Henry knew every one of them and made a mental note to report them to the golf committee.

Wait a minute, he thought. He stopped in his tracks. Brian Houston can't be playing. He's dead! Henry was sure he had seen the obituary in the club newsletter just a couple of weeks ago. The man had a heart attack in a restaurant in Glendale, Henry recalled, and it was rumored he was in the company of a young woman who was definitely not his wife. So what was he doing on the first fairway?

Henry rubbed his eyes and looked again. Brian Houston wasn't there. He scanned the woods on the right side, but he wasn't there either. I must be seeing things, Henry thought. His headache was not as severe, but it was still there. Maybe it was causing hallucinations. He shook it off and hurried to the range.

Rocky was there, but he was deeply occupied with another student, Florence Longstem. Henry waved, but Rocky was intently focused on Florence's healthy chest. Might as well warm up, Henry thought. Maybe I can get his attention when Florence stops swinging her boobs in his face.

Henry's clubs had been set out on the range for the lesson he'd missed, so he stretched a bit and took some tentative practice swings. His head still hurt, but the aspirin must have kicked in because his pain had subsided from skull splitting to more of a dull throb. His eyes didn't work quite right, though, as he found when he addressed the first ball. He blinked hard and squinted until the ball came into focus. Taking a tentative half swing, he made satisfactory contact. He made four more half swings, feeling better and hitting harder each time. He found his vision improved if he turned his head slightly to the right.

That didn't help his hook, though. The first full swing Henry took sent the ball spinning viciously to the left. He took another swipe but the result was the same duck hook that had caused the guys in his regular foursome to start calling him "Hank The Yank." He swung again and again, but each one was worse than the last. Exasperated, he looked up to see if Rocky was available yet. He saw the pro walking off the lesson tee with Florence, her hand tucked lovingly into his back pocket. Henry groaned.

"Looks like your teacher's got a new pet," someone said.

Henry turned. A man smoking a cigarette leaned casually on a golf club behind him. Steely grey eyes appraised Henry from beneath the short brim of a white newsboy's cap. Henry felt like a rabbit being sized up by a hawk. The man wore a trim cardigan and perfectly pleated slacks that broke just right over the tops of gleaming shoes. He was short, but Henry sensed serious power in his relaxed stance. The man could have stepped out of Henry's favorite picture in the locker room.

"You look like Ben Hogan," Henry said.

"That's because I am."

Henry just stared at him. The hallucinations are getting worse, he thought. I really ought to see a doctor. On the other hand, he realized, his head had stopped hurting and his eyes were working right, too. If you could call seeing an apparition of Ben Hogan in front of you "working right."

"Mr. H-H-Hogan!" Henry stammered.

"Call me Ben," Hogan said with a wry smile.

"Gee, thanks, Ben. I'm Henry Harrington."

"I know, Henry." Hogan said. He took a lungful of smoke and nodded down the range as he blew it out. "Having a little trouble with your game lately?"

Henry hung his head. "Yeah, that's why I'm here." He looked up to see Rocky and Florence disappear into the clubhouse in the distance.

"He can't help you anymore," Hogan said. "But I can."

"You mean…?"

"That's right, Henry. I fought a hook for years. I finally found the secret, though. Do you know where?"

Henry thought for a minute, then said, "In the dirt?"

"Good boy," Hogan smiled. "You're absolutely correct."

He wasn't nearly as ice-cold standoffish as usually reported, Henry thought.

"Yes, Henry, the secret is in the dirt. Practice, practice, practice. I hit balls until my hands bled. Then I hit some more. One day, I found the secret." Hogan paused. "I only share it with certain people, though." He peered into Henry's eyes like he was searching for something in the depths of his soul.

Henry blinked in confusion. "Like me?" he asked.

"Could be, Henry. But you have to promise me something."

Henry's head gave a little throb, but he ignored it. He asked, "What's that?"

"You have to promise me you won't let it die from lack of use. If I show you my secret, you'll have to practice it for eternity."

"And if I do, will I hit the ball straight?"

"Forever," Hogan promised.

Hogan's secret! The Holy Grail of golf. Since the man had mentioned it in a *Life Magazine* article, the secret had sparked fevered speculation and an endless stream of charlatans claiming to know how the Hawk controlled the ball better than any player in history. There had been more successful pros on tour, mainly because Hogan often struggled mightily with his putter, but no one had ever struck the ball with such sweet purity. To learn Hogan's secret would be like having Marilyn Monroe privately help you out of your new green jacket after the award ceremony for the Masters.

"Ben, can I ask you something?"

"Sure, Henry. What's on your mind?"

"Why me?"

Hogan nodded as if he expected the question. "There are two reasons. First, it's because you deserve it. When you walked away from that mess in the parking lot, you did it because you weren't going to let anything keep you from working on your game. Isn't that right?"

Henry said, "Yeah, I guess so."

"I like grit in a man, Henry."

"Thanks." Henry was humbled by Hogan's words but wondered if he could live up to his expectations.

"Now watch this—carefully," Hogan said. He flicked his cigarette away and stepped up to a ball. With no wasted motion and smoothness Henry could only dream about, Hogan hit a shot that rose steadily, faded just slightly as it reached its zenith, and landed right in front of the two hundred yard marker. He looked back at Henry expectantly. "What did you notice?" he asked.

Henry shook his head. "That was perfect. But what was I supposed to see?" He half expected Hogan to walk away in disgust.

Instead, Hogan winked at him. "That's just it. No one ever sees it. Somebody once said I cupped my wrist at the top of the swing, but that's no secret—everybody does that if they want to hit a fade. Just like you bow your wrist to hit a draw." He demonstrated by waggling the club both ways in front of Henry, who nodded. He knew that trick.

"Now I'm going to swing real slow," Hogan said. "You'll see the secret if you move back a few steps and watch carefully."

Henry backed up so he could see Hogan's entire body. He concentrated on keeping his mind focused on what Hogan was doing. Again, effortlessly and smoothly, Hogan swung at the ball, this time at half speed.

"I see it!" Henry exclaimed. He did, too. He saw exactly what Hogan did with his swing that no one else could do—at least not intentionally every time. It was so simple and so perfect. Henry's smile went from ear to ear, as did Hogan's.

"You saw it, didn't you?" Hogan asked.

"I did!" Henry answered. "It's beautiful. And I can do it, too. I just need to practice."

Then Henry remembered something else and grew somber. "Ben, you said there were two reasons."

Again, Hogan nodded. "I like you, Henry. You pay attention." He gave Henry a bracing stare. "The second reason is that I know you'll never tell anyone else. You know that, don't you?"

Henry let the words soak in for a moment until he understood what Hogan meant. The ugly incident in the parking lot came flooding back. Henry had jumped out of his car, late for his lesson. He dashed for the clubhouse and right into the path of a speeding delivery van. There was a flash of blinding light. A crack of thunder in his skull. Then nothing.

But that wasn't the end. Henry remembered a woozy struggle to his feet. A crowd of people who ignored him as he pushed through them. He stumbled into the locker room unseen by Pepe. Somehow he made his way to the lesson tee only to watch his teacher walk away with another student.

The range was filling up with other players, Henry noticed. He recognized a few of them, mostly older members he remembered from the days when he first joined the club. There were many others he didn't know. Some were dressed in natty pleated slacks and cardigans from Ben Hogan's era. A few wore knickers, knee socks, and long-sleeved shirts with vests and ties. A man at the end of the practice tee tipped his straw boater when Henry looked his way.

"It's just like in the movie," Henry said as much to himself as to Hogan.

"What's that?" Hogan asked.

"I see dead people."

Lost Ball At Hemlock Hills

Bud figured the grit under his eyelids would go away about the same time as the crick in his neck, which would be sometime while he was walking from the first green to the second tee. If I could only sleep stretched flat instead of cramped up in the back seat of the car, he thought, I could possibly par the first hole. It would sure be nice to start a round with some score besides one over. That was one of the special hazards of Pine Forge Municipal Golf Course—you slept in your car in the parking lot if you wanted a tee-time. Then you played your round with a crick in your back or worse.

Bud got in line in front of the pro shop, his place determined by his car's slot in the parking lot, and signed up for next week's time as soon as the shop opened. Then he went back to the parking lot to meet the rest of the foursome. He found Jonesy and Smack perched on a car bumper changing their shoes.

"Where's Tom?" Bud asked.

"He called this morning and cancelled. Said his mother-in-law died in the middle of the night," Smack said.

"That's a shame," Bud said.

"No big deal. He said missing eighteen holes was a small price to pay for a lifetime of peace and quiet," Jonesy said.

"Yeah," Smack laughed. "Then I reminded him that mere death did not excuse him from taking his turn sleeping in the parking lot next week."

"Well, come on," Bud said. "We've got the number six slot. I'll go tell the starter he can make a stand-by happy this morning."

The wait-listed golfer they met at the starter's shack introduced himself as Treat. His bag was a little ratty and his pull cart was past due for a 20,000-mile checkup, but he seemed to know his way around the tee box. His drive landed in the right rough a few yards behind Tom's. It looked like Treat was just another muni hacker. He'd fit in fine.

It turned into a typical Saturday morning. The grass was wet, the greens were dotted with mower clippings, and the first bottleneck of the day was on the second hole, an uphill par three with a canted green and a nasty trap on the left front. If someone in the first group of the day decided to read his bogey putt from every angle, plumb-bob it, take three practice strokes, then step away and start over, a small convention would assemble on the second tee. Bud's was only the sixth group of the morning but there were already two foursomes waiting to tee off when they came off the first green.

"Gonna be one of those days," Jonesy said.

"Yep. You can tell it's Saturday," Smack added. "The second tee looks like the checkout line at the liquor store on payday."

It took well over two and a half hours to play the front nine. There was either a big two-dollar Nassau going on in the first group or somebody up ahead was taking detours into the woods to look for lost balls. Bud would be the first to admit that patience was not his strong suit. He was known to fume if he couldn't hit away as soon as he came up to his ball. It didn't help his game. Treat made small talk as they slogged through the first nine holes, but fortunately he wasn't a chatterbox. He made the turn at five over, two strokes better than the best of the other three. In short, he was a perfectly adequate substitute member of the foursome. He walked with Bud down the tenth fairway where they had both pulled their drives dangerously close to the fairway bunker on the left.

"I don't like to complain," he said. "But is it this slow all the time?"

"Oh yeah," Bud replied. "Sundays are worse."

"Don't they have a ranger?"

"Sure. Don't you remember seeing him on the fourth hole? He was the guy sleeping in the cart parked under the tree on the left."

"Right. Gotcha."

They waited for the green to clear, then played their second shots, Treat's landing short of the green and Bud's to the left.

"Looks like it'll be at least a five-hour round," Bud said. Treat didn't say anything more about the pace of play until the sixteenth hole, another par three. This one was downhill across a creek that ran in front of the green. There was a hillock that blocked part of the view of the creek from the tee. They could see a group looking there for some-body's tee shot while two foursomes waited on the tee.

"Look, you guys," Treat said as they waited behind the tee. "Why don't you come play the course I've been playing the last couple of months. It's brand new—no crowds. Beautiful course, too."

"Where is it?" Jonesy said. "Montana? Must be. I never heard of any course like that around here."

"Like I said, it's new. It's called Hemlock Hills and it's just up the road a piece. This rich guy named Walachian built it in the woods way off Route 23."

"So how come I never heard of it before?" Smack wanted to know.

"It's real private. Walachian doesn't like crowds. Built it mostly to play with some of his rich friends." His voice dropped so the other group on the tee couldn't hear. "He lets a few regular guys like us play when he gets hungry for company. Doesn't charge anything, either, but you have to hire a caddie. Actually, I caddie there too, every once in awhile, just to pick up a little extra."

"This is sounding weirder by the minute," Jonesy said.

"Yeah, and better by the minute, too," Bud added. "What are you doing on this goat track if you can play there?"

"He closes it off now and then so he can play a practice round by himself," Treat said. "But, what the heck, it's his candy store, right? So tell me, do you want to get on the course?" The assent was unanimous.

* * *

The muni foursome couldn't believe the course. They looked down the perfectly manicured first fairway and didn't see anybody ahead of them. There was no starter, no crowd on the practice green, no other cars in the tiny parking lot. It looked like they had the entire magnificent course to themselves. That was not surprising, considering that the entrance road was unmarked. It looked like a private driveway off of Route 23.

"Ready, boys?" Treat asked once they had a chance to soak up the atmosphere and come back to earth. Treat carried two bags and another caddie, Sandy, took the other two. "There is only one local rule at Hemlock Hills," he said. "You must find any lost balls. No matter where it goes, you have to find it. Mr. Walachian doesn't like to see them when he walks in the woods." The four men exchanged glances and shrugged.

"No problem," Smack said. "Jonesy knows his way around the woods real well. He spends half the round in the trees anyway." Everybody laughed except the caddies.

"Usual game?" Tom asked, holding out his cap to collect the other players' balls.

"Yep, let's do it," Jonesy said. He reached in and pulled out Bud's ball and the teams were determined. Smack tossed a tee in the air and Bud was first up. He looked down the fairway with determination, stepped up to his ball, and drove it right down the middle.

"Jeez, where'd this guy come from?" Tom said.

"That's my partner!" Jonesy said. His drive landed within six feet of Bud's. The other two tee shots went to the same place as if guided by radar.

"I think I'm gonna like this place," Smack said as they walked off the tee. He was away by a few feet and landed his second shot in the middle of the green. The others followed. As Tom sank a twelve-footer for birdie, the level of excitement went up accordingly.

"That's it," Bud exclaimed as they walked to the second tee. "I'm here for life. Think Mr. Walachian would let me move in?" Sandy and Treat exchanged glances.

A little seriously, Treat asked, "Wouldn't your wife miss you?"

"He spends so much time on the course now his wife demands a picture ID before she'll let him see the kids," Smack said.

"Hey! Just because she made me wear a name tag to our anniversary party. . ." Bud protested.

* * *

The men played the next ten holes much the same. The course couldn't have been better, the weather more perfect. Not a soul held them up, hit into them, or picked up one of their balls "by accident" in an adjacent fairway. Tom and Smack won the front side one up, and no one in the foursome shot worse than two over par. They were all playing way over their heads. Bud and Jonesy won the tenth, but Tom and Smack pulled ahead again by winning the eleventh hole. They loved every second of it.

Tom's drive on the long par-five twelfth hole cruised thirty yards farther than usual and rolled another fifteen to come to rest on the right side of the fairway next to a large bunker.

"My God. I think you hit that ball three hundred yards!" Jonesy said.

"That's what partners are for!" Smack shouted. Then he drove his own ball a couple of yards just short of Tom's.

"All right, all ready!" Bud exclaimed. "Didn't you guys hear? Steroids are illegal." His drive landed in the bunker and Jonesy's ended up in the short rough on the left. Tom and Smack whistled a happy tune walking down the fairway. Bud looked through the trees to the still-deserted first hole.

"Man. It's like we're the only humans on the planet," he said.

"You may well be the only ones on the course," Treat answered. They waited while Jonesy played. His shot rolled to the front of the green—a near impossibility under normal circumstances but truly extraordinary given that he was playing from the rough.

"Now who needs a steroid check!" Smack said. Emboldened by his partner's success, Bud played a five wood from the sand and flew it into a greenside bunker. "You know," Smack observed, "I hear steroids are bad for the brain, too." His second shot landed in front of the green with Jonesy, but Tom pured a five iron to the center, less than fifteen feet from the hole.

"Yeoow!" Tom cried and they practically ran up to the green.

Sandy smiled at Treat. "Looks like my guy's on fire," he said.

"I have a feeling one of mine's going to make a run at him," Treat answered.

Bud got up from the trap but two-putted for a par. Jonesy and Smack both chipped close for easy birdies. Tom rolled in his putt as casually as if he made natural eagles every day. The other three howled.

Tom's drive on the thirteenth hole, a dog-leg right, was even better than his bomb on the second hole. It cut the corner and landed dead center in the fairway an easy sand wedge from the green. Smack and Jonesy hit the fairway at the dog leg twenty-five yards behind Tom.

"I've had about enough of this," Bud said in mock ferocity as he teed up his ball. The other three exchanged knowing glances.

"It's Goldilocks time," Smack said.

"Yeah. This is when Bud goes to play in the woods with the bears," Jonesy chuckled.

"You just watch," Bud said as he settled over the ball. He drew the club head back slowly, cranked way past parallel at the top, then unwound like Sammy Sosa swinging for the fences. As his ball rocketed on a rising trajectory down the fairway, he turned to face his smug gallery. "Whaddya think about that?" he smirked. Smack, whose eyes hadn't left the ball, started snickering. Bud turned back just in time to see his ball take a hard right and disappear into the trees. He groaned while the rest of the group laughed mercilessly.

"Cut that corner a little close, didn't you partner?" Jonesy cackled.

Quietly, Treat said, "Guess you're going into the woods."

Treat left Jonesy's bag on the fairway with his ball, then followed Bud as he trudged toward the woods. "I think I know where it is," Treat said. "You guys stay here." Sandy made no move to join the hunt, so the other three men didn't either.

As soon as Bud stepped from the long grass into the trees, it got dark; far darker than it should be at that time of day. It was cold, too, like he had just stepped into an over-air-conditioned bar. A twig crackled behind him and his heart jumped into his throat. He twirled around, but it was just Treat.

"We'll find it before Mr. Walachian does," Treat said cheerfully. "It should be over here." He pointed further into the trees.

"Uh, sure," Bud said as his pulse slowed to something closer to normal. He walked further into the woods, which seemed to get colder and darker with every step. They pushed through a little undergrowth, then came to a stand of giant hemlocks where the ground was kept clear by a carpet of needles. The hemlocks were so thick it was dark as night underneath them. It was so cold Bud's breath fogged in front of his face.

"It's like a meat locker in here," he said. He looked up only to see Treat disappearing among the thick tree trunks. Not wanting to be left alone, Bud hurried after him.

"I think I got it!" Treat finally called out. Bud could barely see him in the gloom. Treat had put the bag down and was pointing to the ground up ahead. Bud let loose a deep sigh of relief. He hadn't noticed that he had been holding his breath.

"Do I have a shot!" he called.

"I think so!" Treat yelled back.

When Bud got there, he saw the ball lying on the hemlock needles in a small clearing, but it was surround by a wall of trees. "I thought you said I had a shot!" Bud looked quizzically at the caddie. Just then another man slipped into the clearing from the direction of the hole. He wore black plus-fours, black shoes, and a black sweater vest over a long-sleeved white shirt with a wine-colored tie. As he came closer, Bud could see that the shirt had a small brown stain on the collar.

"Bud," Treat said solemnly, "May I present our host, Mr. Walachian. Mr. Walachian, this is Bud."

"How do you do?" Walachian extended his hand while his discomfiting eyes bored into Bud's. His hand was clammy in Bud's grip.

"Great!" Bud said. "I mean, nice to meetchya."

"I hope you are enjoying Hemlock Hills," Mr. Walachian said, holding on firmly to Bud's hand. Maybe it was the uncertain light filtering through the trees, but Bud felt strangely light headed.

"Oh, yeah! This place is great. Thanks a lot for letting us play."

"The pleasure is all mine, I assure you." The dark man turned to the caddie. "I think Bud should hit a seven iron from here, don't you, Treat?"

"Sounds right to me, Mr. Walachian." Treat drew the club from the bag, but handed it to the dark man instead of to Bud. Without another word, he hoisted Bud's bag onto his shoulder and disappeared into the trees in the direction of the fairway. Bud was left alone with the strange owner of the course, who still gripped his hand.

"Hey wait!" Bud called after Treat but the caddie was gone.

"Don't worry, Bud," Mr. Walachian said softly. "I have just what you need to make this shot." Bud finally pulled his hand free.

"What shot?" he said. "I can't even see the sky, much less the green." The dark man gestured over his shoulder with the seven iron.

"I think you can snake one through that opening. Don't you?" he said.

"What open...." Bud's jaw dropped as his eyes followed the pointing seven iron to a ten-yard-wide alley through the trees that lead directly to the green a hundred and eighty yards away. The flag flapped easily in a slight breeze, sun light glinting on the stick. "Where'd that come from?" he gulped.

"Why, it's been there all along, Bud. You just needed a little help from me to see it." He moved uncomfortably closer and pressed the seven iron into Bud's hands. "I can help you do a lot of things." The club vibrated softly and Bud immediately became calm. He looked back down the alley through the trees.

"Like laser this seven iron one-eighty through that chute?" he asked.

"Certainly. And much, much more." The man stepped even closer until his chest touched Bud's arm. His chin was practically in Bud's ear. If Bud turned, he would be kissing Mr. Walachian's pale lips.

"How would you like to become a member at Hemlock Hills? To play whenever you want?" he whispered into Bud's ear. "No more overnights in the parking lot. No more five hour rounds." Mr. Walachian crooned Bud's tune.

"Who do I have to kill?" he asked, his gaze never leaving the flagstick beyond the trees.

"Actually. . ." Mr. Walachian paused as if to think about it. "No one. But we'll get to that. I can also help you become a scratch player, my friend. What do you say?"

"You do that, buddy, and I'll not only join your club, I'll mow the fairways on my day off and clean the locker room toilets on Sunday." Bud's eyes shone as he envisioned himself standing on the first tee resplendent in his own plus-fours. He'd wear red, though, definitely bright red.

"That won't be necessary," Mr. Walachian chuckled, "although I appreciate the offer. I have another small service in mind." Bud turned his head and stared deep into the man's eyes. Their noses were nearly touching.

"Scratch, huh?" he said, thinking about it.

"Forever," Mr. Walachian said. "All I ask in return is that you introduce me to new prospective members from time to time."

"You can make me scratch?" Bud asked again. Mr. Walachian nodded and Bud's eyes narrowed. "Prove it."

"With pleasure." Mr. Walachian smiled like a wolf meeting Red Riding Hood's grandmother. "Here's your first lesson: I want you to take your normal backswing, but pause motionless at the top just long enough to say 'eternity' before you swing through."

"Eternity, huh?" Bud said. He lined up and took his stance, stole a last look down the alley, and swung exactly as instructed. The seven iron made soundless contact with the ball and Bud held a picture-perfect follow-through as his eyes followed it into the air. The ball rose through the trees in lazy slow motion. It gleamed white when it broke into the sun above the trees, then it floated softly onto the green, bounced once, and rolled into the cup.

"Welcome to Hemlock Hills," Mr. Walachian whispered.

"Ahhh." Bud released his breath in a long, satiated sigh. "How sweet it is to be a member," he said.

"You have no idea," Mr. Walachian answered. His long white teeth glistened as he turned back the collar of Bud's shirt.

As Time Goes By

"Again! You're playing golf again today!?" Myron's wife slammed the newspaper down on the breakfast table and glared at him incredulously.

"It's such a beautiful day," he replied as he steadied his coffee cup. "Hate to waste the opportunity to play."

"Opportunity!" she moaned. You played yesterday! And the day before! And the day before that!"

"Now, Loretta, you know the doctor said the exercise is good for my condition," Myron said as he wiped up slopped coffee with his napkin.

"You want exercise? Try doing something around this house for a change. You know, mow the lawn, clean out the garage, little things like that."

"I will, dear, I promise," he replied. "I have your list of chores and I'll start on them right away. This afternoon. Right after my round. I promise." Myron gave her his most sincere smile and got up from the table. His wife sighed.

It was an old, old argument that flared every time he played two days in a row. Myron didn't understand the problem, even though his wife explained it to him—frequently. The way he looked at it, there were only so many good days every year and you should make the best of them by doing something you really enjoyed, like playing golf. He worked hard at his job and he deserved his leisure time. Mowing the lawn would wait. Life is short. You should relish every minute of it. Loretta didn't exactly see things this way.

"Even if you're not going to take care of the house, I wish you'd spend less time on the golf course and more time with your son," she said.

"We have a son?" he said in mock surprise, trying to ease the tension with a little joke.

"Oh, Myron, that's not funny." Sadly, she shook her head.

As Myron got in his car, he noticed the paint peeling on the dark green shutters on the house and there was a little something growing out of the gutters. Guess they need to be cleaned out, he thought. An overgrown forsythia scraped the passenger side of his car as he swerved to avoid his son's tricycle sitting in the driveway. Better trim that bush back, too, he thought. By the time Myron pulled his trusty Buick into the parking lot at Fairdale Golf Club, though, the list of mundane chores had been banished to the back of his mind and he was focused on a glorious day on the course.

A magnificent spring day it was, too. Still-new pale green leaves sprouted on the trees and the light breeze carried just a hint of summer heat to come. Gauzy white clouds drifted across the sky. They drifted a little fast, though, Myron thought. Maybe there was a storm blowing in from somewhere. No need to worry about today though. The weatherman said it was supposed to be beautifully clear all day.

"Myron!" the starter greeted him as he walked through the clubhouse. "What a surprise! Haven't seen you for almost twenty-four hours!"

"Hi ya, Johnnie," Myron said. "Thought I'd squeeze in a quick round today, too."

"Tough work, but somebody's got to do it, right?"

"There you go," Myron said. "My thoughts exactly." Johnnie put him with a threesome just getting ready to tee off. They all looked to be about Myron's age and, judging by their tee shots, they all played at about the same less-than-spectacular but still respectable level. He gathered from their banter that they all worked together as accountants in an insurance office downtown. Hearing the weather forecast the night before, they'd called in sick.

"What a great day!" one of the men exclaimed as they started walking down the first fairway.

"Any day on the course is a great day," Myron offered. There was hearty assent.

The pleasure of the round built on itself hole after hole. The four men were pretty evenly matched, but nobody really cared who was beating whom anyway. Myron just barely kept track of his strokes because he was busy taking in the wonders of the day.

His enjoyment became almost orgasmic at the par three fourteenth, the signature hole at Fairdale. The tiny green snuggled into a hillside 170 yards from the tee, protected by a pristine pond in the left front but approachable by the timid via a safe landing area on the right. Flower beds dotting the hillside behind the green put on such a spectacular seasonal show that the hole forced the golfer to literally stop and smell the flowers. There was a slight breeze in their face and the first of the three accountants caught his tee shot fat. His ball plopped into the water twenty yards short of the green. The other two played it safe and went to the right side.

Myron, though, didn't play golf in order to see how many balls he had left at the end of the day. He loved the way the ball clicked almost imperceptibly against the club face right in the middle of a well-oiled swing. He played for the unadulterated joy that comes from watching a well-struck ball float gently into the blue sky. Flirting with penalty strokes simply heightened the sensation much the way an illicit partner enhances an orgasm. Myron took one extra club to compensate for the breeze, swung smoothly, and clipped his shot just a little thin. The ball flew directly over the pin, bounced once on the back of the green, and nestled down in a flower bed on the hillside behind.

A local rule dictated that Myron retrieve his ball from the flowers and play his next shot penalty-free from a drop area. As he bent to pluck his ball from under the dense leaves of a blooming peony, a perfect bud moved in the breeze and caught his eye. It quivered, stopped, then quivered again. Then the soft, moist petals unfolded and stretched slowly into a glorious pink and white display as if captured by time-lapse photography. The phenomenon left Myron speechless with wonder.

"Hellooo! Earth to Myron!" broke his reverie. It was one of the accountants. They were all on the green waiting for him to chip on.

"Sorry, guys," he said. "I guess I zoned out for a minute there." He chipped close, putted out, and they all moved to the next tee.

* * *

It was inexplicably blistering summer hot by the time Myron and the accountants walked off the eighteenth green. Myron shook hands all around and headed into the grill for a cold beer while they scuttled off to their cars, discussing how—or whether—they were going to sneak into the office today. Myron's beer was cold and crisp, the frosty glass itself refreshing to the touch. Maybe I'll have a quick burger, he thought, then go home and trim back that forsythia by the driveway. In fact, maybe I'll just cut it down altogether, he thought with pleasure. Myron hated that bush.

Just as Myron stuffed the last bite of juicy cheeseburger into his mouth, two old codgers hiked into the grill. He heard them grumbling at the bar about some other old guy who'd had the temerity to forego this afternoon's round to attend a funeral.

"He could have left right after the church service and skipped the graveside crap. Still make the tee time that way," one of them growled.

"Yeah, it was only his brother-in-law, for crying out loud," the other one said.

"That's the source of the problem," the first old guy jumped back in. "He's whipped, I'm telling you. Absolutely pussy whipped."

The other one said, "Shame he's going to miss such a perfect day."

Myron drained the last of this beer. "Excuse me, fellas," he said from his seat at the bar. "If you need a third, I'm looking for a game this afternoon." The two men looked at each other and shrugged encouragingly.

"Glad to have you, pal," one said. "Long as none of your wife's relatives are starring in a funeral this afternoon." The other man chuckled and Myron joined in.

"Just let me call home first to make sure," he laughed. The two old golfers went silent. "Haha. Just kidding," Myron quickly added. "I just want to let me wife know I won't be home this afternoon." They released their collective breath.

Fairdale is one of those progressive courses that not only prohibits cell phones on the course, but bans them from the premises entirely. For those golfers who absolutely had to be in touch with the real world, there was a pay phone in the grill room. Myron was somewhat irritated to find, though, that it now required four quarters—a whole buck—to make a local call! This deregulation thing is out of control, he thought as he listened to the phone ring at home. He was startled back to reality by a slightly new outgoing message on his answering machine and thought for just a moment that the woman's voice delivering it wasn't Loretta's. But he lost his train of thought when the beep demanded he speak and he left a brief apologetic message saying that he was going to play another round but should be home for dinner. Mostly, he felt relieved that he didn't have to deliver that message in person.

The sweltering heat had eased by the time the three men got on the first tee. Again, Myron noticed that the low white clouds were whipping rather fast across the horizon. They made a stunning backdrop for the first fairway, which stretched invitingly before him. He filled his lungs with the smell of warm grass.

"It's a great day, isn't it!" he exclaimed as he put his tee in the ground and balanced his ball on top of it.

"Any day on the course is a great day," one of the men answered. Myron sent his drive right down the middle of the fairway, slightly further than where he'd driven it that morning. He was relaxed, warmed up, and well-fed. Myron sensed a good round coming on.

And it was a good round. He made the turn just three over par—a fine performance considering he'd sent his tee shot out of bounds on the sixth hole. His two companions wheezed around the course a little bit, but they didn't slow him down at all. In fact, Myron got a little extra spring in his step every time he drove his ball thirty yards beyond theirs. Interesting connection, he thought. He wondered if their age differential matched the distance difference one for one—one yard for each year. He stowed that idea for consideration later so he could focus on enjoying the rest of the afternoon.

There was no question that either of his companions was going to go for the pin on the fourteenth hole. They both hit fairway woods safely to the landing area on the right. Remembering how he had hit over the green in the morning round, and feeling a little helping breeze, Myron took one club less. He executed a perfect swing but, was dismayed to see his tee shot strike the front edge of the green and bounce back into the pond.

"Damn," he said. "Must be getting tired."

"Maybe you're weakening in your old age," joshed one of his playing partners.

"You gotta watch out," Cackled the other one. "Time sneaks up on you."

Myron reloaded and hit again, even though he could have used the drop area. This time, his ball landed a couple of feet further onto the green and rolled toward the hole instead of back into the water. He felt vindicated even though the second shot was no prize, either. As he walked onto the green to mark his ball, Myron noticed that the peonies he'd admired on the morning were no longer in bloom. Strangely, though, black-eyed Susans, normally a late summer bloomer, dominated the hillside flower beds behind the green. He didn't remember any there this morning. They don't appear to be doing as well, he thought, noticing that the ground beneath them was littered with yellow petals and their normally dark green foliage was turning brown.

"Hey Myron!" one of the old guys yelled from the right of the green. "You gonna mark you ball or stare at the daisies?"

"Sorry, boys," Myron called back as he snapped back to the present. "I was just noticing something. Don't you think it's a little early in the season for Black-eyed Susans to be blooming?"

"Susans, schmoosans," one of the old golfers replied. "We spent thirty years in an insurance office. What do we know about flowers?" Insurance office? Myron was struck by the coincidence, but didn't say anything because the old boys were starting to huff impatiently. He marked his ball and stepped aside.

As it does late every afternoon, the day turned to dusk. As Myron and the two men played the last four holes, it also got sharply cooler as the sun dipped behind the low speeding clouds on the western horizon. If he hadn't known better, Myron would have sworn he felt a bit of autumn chill in the breeze that brushed his face as he loaded his clubs into the trunk of the car. There were only a couple of cars still in the parking lot at that hour, but they both made Myron's Buick look old—real old—by comparison. There was a strange Toyota parked three spaces away that looked like something Arnold Schwartzenegger might drive in a science fiction movie. Guess I ought to think about trading in the old girl, he thought.

Out of habit, Myron swung wide to avoid the forsythia as he turned into his driveway. He almost drove off the driveway onto the lawn, though, when he realized the bush wasn't there! He got out of the Buick and ran back to see the spot where the bush used to stand. It was as grassy smooth as the rest of the lawn! He looked at the house, thinking maybe he'd pulled into the wrong driveway while woolgathering. But, no, it was the right house. At least he thought so. But then he noticed the shutters. Someone had painted them today! No, he thought, my eyes must be fooling me in the dusk. Loretta could have hired somebody to remove that bush on short notice, but nobody was going to paint those shutters in one day.

Still wondering what had gone on around the house while he was at the course, Myron got back in the Buick and clicked the remote to open the garage door. Nothing happened. Damn batteries, he thought. He trudged to the front door and put his key in the lock. It wouldn't turn. Myron wondered again if he was at the wrong house, but no, there was the mailbox with his number on it right down at the end of the driveway where it belonged.

A child laughed inside the house as Myron rang the doorbell. A strange young woman opened the door. A vaguely familiar little boy peeked out from behind her legs.

"Yes?" she asked. "May I help you?"

Myron didn't know what to say, nor did he want to just barge through the door past her, since she was partially blocking it as would anybody who had just opened their door to find a stranger on the step.

"Hey, Dad!" the kid yelled over his shoulder back into the house. "It's the guy in the picture!"

"Hush," the woman said, then looked at Myron expectantly. He finally found his voice, although it didn't work very well.

"I, uh, I uh," he stammered. "Who are you?" he finally spit out.

"I'm sorry," she said, "but I don't know you and. . . ." She pushed the kid back and started to close the door.

"I live here!" Myron finally spurted out.

"Robert!" she called to someone in the house as she closed the door firmly in Myron's face. "You better come here!" Myron heard her say. Myron stood on his front step totally confused. Before he could decide what to do, the door was snapped open by a young man who looked so much like the familiar little boy that he had to be his father. The man, too, looked like someone Myron knew.

"What do you. . ." he started to demand, then swallowed. "Dad?" he asked. Myron squinted and peered closely into the man's face. He uttered his son's name just before he passed out.

Myron came awake on the sofa with his son hovering over him and a boy who was evidently his grandson still peeking at him from behind his mother's knees. Could she be his daughter-in-law? He struggled to sit upright. "What's going on?" he stammered. "How did I get here?"

Ignoring Myron's questions, Robert asked, "What happened to you, Dad? Where did you go?"

"Go! I just went to play a round of golf this morning," Myron answered. "Then I decided to play another round after lunch. It was such a perfect day! Would have been a shame to waste it. Didn't your mother get my message?" Myron stopped and looked around. "Say, where is your mother?"

"Mom's been gone for years, now, Dad," Robert said solemnly.

"Gone?"

"Yes, she passed."

Myron let that sink in. Loretta was dead. It had been such a weird day. Now this. He wasn't sure what to do or say next. He looked at his hands, at his shoes, at his now-grown son who stared back at him in wonderment. He considered the possibilities. Finally, Myron shifted on the sofa and said softly. "Can I stay here tonight?" Robert looked at his wife, who nodded uncertainly.

"Don't worry," Myron said. "I won't be any bother. You won't even know I was here. I'll leave at the crack of dawn. I should be able to get an early tee time."

Bonus Excerpt from

HUNTING ELF

A doggone Christmas story

Hunting Elf

Chapter 1

Dan McCoy's fingers froze on the door knob, his hand stilled by an unholy cacophony of snarls, barks, and growls coming from somewhere inside his darkened house. He swore it sounded like a pack of wild jackals that had been aroused by the sound of his key in the lock. Dan had never really heard a pack of wild jackals, but he was sure this is exactly what they would sound like if one ever invaded his house. As he cautiously turned the doorknob, though, he realized he heard only one snarling beast, not a dozen. Whatever it was, it howled ferociously, desperately longing to tear out Dan's throat with its yellowed, dripping fangs. For some reason, that image reminded Dan of his mother-in-law.

When the cab let Dan out a minute earlier, the house was dark except for the Christmas tree in the front window. It twinkled a "welcome home" he was very glad to see. It was late Friday night and Dan was tired. He was returning home from Cleveland where he had spent the last three days running a seminar on employee motivation for a group of accountants. His plane into LaGuardia had been late that night, and the car service he always used—because they were so dependable—wasn't there when he got off the plane. By the time he stood in line and got a cab to Harrington, the New York suburb where he lived, he had missed the neighborhood Christmas caroling party. He briefly considered catching the last few minutes of the soirée, it was just down the block, but his feet painfully reminded him that he had been standing on them for a long, long time. They insisted it was time to rest, so he trudged up the walk, put his key in the door, and turned the knob.

The noise level went up as Dan warily pulled the door open. He remembered that his wife, June, had bought a Silky Terrier puppy to give to her mother for Christmas. It was going to be a surprise replacement for the treasured family pet that had passed away that fall after a sad, lingering illness. Esther, Dan's mother-in-law, insisted that she didn't want another dog, but that meant nothing to her daughter, who was determined to make her mother happy whether she wanted to be or not. Dan loved his wife deeply, but he had to admit she sometimes stepped over the line when it came to determination.

The insane barking continued while he hung his overcoat in the closet. He left his suit bag and briefcase in the hall and walked cautiously into the kitchen where the puppy was assiduously trying to escape the travel crate where June had left him while she went to the party. Dan peeked into the crate and saw two shiny black eyes staring back out at him from under a mop of disheveled hair. He couldn't believe that something not much bigger than a penny loafer could make that much noise. The pup looked out at Dan and saw a trim middle-aged man in a navy blue suit peering through bifocals and wearing an inquisitive look on his face. The man had light brown hair peppered with gray at the temples and a jaw line that was thinking about forming jowls. As soon as the pup saw his opponent, he quieted down and sat silently on his haunches, waiting for Dan's next move.

There was a note on the kitchen counter. "Dear Dan, This is Elf. Keep in crate. Home around ten. Love, June." Cute name, he thought. "Elf" is just right for a Christmas present with pointy, tufted ears and sparkly eyes surrounded by a fright wig of tan, black and silver hair. The puppy was obviously high-spirited and probably playful, and he would look wickedly cute in a little red Santa hat and jingle bell collar, which was the kind of thing June would make him wear Christmas morning. The little puppy sat quietly in the crate while Dan considered June's note. Hmmm. She probably means he's a little frisky, Dan thought. The warning note notwithstanding, he wasn't worried about this cute little puppy. A quick scratch behind the ears and maybe a doggie treat, and Dan would have a friend for life. So he opened the crate door.

But Elf didn't stick around to get acquainted. He shot out of that crate like a comet with hair. The pup hurtled twice around the kitchen and disappeared past Dan's legs in a streak down the hall. He skidded on the hardwood floor, made a sharp left turn, and disappeared up the stairs. Dan started laughing at the puppy's antics, but then it dawned on him that Elf was almost certainly not house-broken. Maybe June's note should have been more specific! He jumped to his feet and raced up the stairs himself. Dan caught Elf on the bed in the master bedroom just as a robust yellow stream poured between the puppy's legs and onto Dan's pillow.

"You son of a gun!" Dan shouted as he dove across the bed. He scooped up the dog just before Elf stopped peeing and a warm dribble ran under Dan's watch band. A yellow puddle slowly seeped into his pillow. A fierce urge to strangle the dog surged through Dan, but he took a deep breath and his better nature won out. Besides, they couldn't very well give June's mother a dead puppy for Christmas.

"Bad dog! Potty outside!" he scolded sternly. He pushed Elf's face into the fresh stain on the pillow, smacked him lightly on the nose, and carried the squirming little criminal downstairs toward the back door. He had read somewhere that the first rule of dog discipline is that no bad deed should go unpunished. In the case of "accidents" like this one, the perpetrator should go immediately outside while the crime is still fresh in his mind.

Dan slid open the patio door and started to put the miscreant down on the patio, but then he came to his senses and looked around for a leash. The yard was partially fenced, but there were plenty of escape holes for a creature less than twelve inches tall. Elf must have read his mind, because he chose that moment to put his whole four-pound self into a tremendous lurch out of Dan's arms. The dog's feet barely touched the floor before he was out the open door and gone into the darkness.

"I should have throttled him when I had the chance," Dan fumed. He hit the light switch, but the little bulb illuminated only about six feet of patio immediately outside the door, leaving the rest of the small yard in blackness. A picket fence ran along both sides of the yard, with gates on either side of the house. The back boundary of the yard was a steep drop-off into a rock garden that slanted down at an impossible grade away from the house. A thin hedge along the top closed in that side of the lawn. The hedge line was broken by a gate leading to a stone stairway that curved down through the garden.

A dog-shaped blur sped through the darkness toward the left side of the house just outside the circle of light. Dan dashed to cut it off and their paths would have met at the corner of the house, but Elf saw him coming and wheeled to shoot across the yard just out of reach. He streaked toward the opposite corner where the fence on the right side met the hedge along the back. Dan made a snap turn that sent a twinge up his back. He shook it off and got to mid-yard in three strides, where he stopped abruptly because the dog was coming in his direction! He could just barely make out the puppy's tiny body moving along the hedge. Dan crept stealthily forward, not wanting to panic the dog any more than he already had. Elf ignored him, though, and kept his pointy nose to the ground sniffing intently along the base of the hedge. Then he stepped into the bushes and disappeared.

Dan lunged through the hedge after him, forgetting that the property fell off steeply into the rock garden on the other side. Fortunately, he didn't take a header down the hill but sort of skied over the mulch on the leather soles of his shoes instead. Somehow, he managed to halt precariously in mid-slide and stay on his feet. As he caught his breath, he realized that shoving through hedges and skidding over the stalks of wintering perennials was bound to give his nice navy-blue suit a few wrinkles. Just then, the puppy scampered up the hill past him and disappeared through the hedge back into the yard. Dan lurched after him, but his feet flew out from under and he slid helplessly the rest of the way to the bottom of the garden, wiping out a wide swatch of plants and several rocks with his backside. So much for his suit.

Now Dan was mad. His elbow hurt, his butt hurt, and his ego hurt, all bruised by that over-excited bottle brush of a dog. He stomped up the stone steps two at a time. He spied Elf panting in the circle of light at the back door.

"Come here, you little bastard!" he shouted, leaping toward the patio. Elf darted for the fence, poked his head between the pickets, and wriggled through. But Dan was right behind him. He fell to his knees and stuck his arm between the pickets. "Gotcha!" he crowed triumphantly as his fingers closed on the pup's neck. But, as Dan knelt grimly gripping the dog through the fence with one hand, he realized they were stymied; Elf couldn't get away, but Dan couldn't get him back between the pickets either, at least, not without dismembering him. As attractive as that option seemed, Dan knew it wasn't a viable solution. He clenched the wriggling dog firmly and tried to ignore the dampness seeping into his knees while he tried to figure out what to do. There was an airy feeling in the seat of his pants and his shirt had a rip in the sleeve where it was snagged between the pickets. But none of this mattered at the moment. If I can just shift my grip and aim the dog's head this way, he thought, I can pull him back through the fence. The little pup was quiet and motionless under his hand, waiting to see what the man was going to do next. Dan carefully reached through with his other arm to turn him around and aim his head back toward the fence. As he switched hands on the dog's neck, his grip loosened ever so slightly. Sensing opportunity, Elf squirmed out of his grasp and disappeared into the night.

Dan was left with his arms stuck between the pickets. He looked like a convict in a bad prison movie reaching through the bars to plead for clemency as the executioner approached. And just like a condemned prisoner, Dan sensed doom as he peered through the fence into the empty darkness; he had just lost his mother-in-law's Christmas present.

Dan McCoy didn't deserve execution. He was a good guy just trying to get along in life. His neighbors knew him as a friendly sort always ready to help move a piece of furniture or loan you his lawn mower. His clients not only respected him, they liked him, too, which made his consulting business steady if not overly prosperous. He was good to his wife, obedient as a rule, and he even got along pretty well with his mother-in-law. Dan got into a little trouble now and then, usually because of some half-baked idea cooked up over a beer with his neighbor, Jerry, but it was never anything that couldn't be patched up with a call to a repairman or a heartfelt apology to their wives. In other words, Dan was harmless; just a guy doing his best to do the right thing in life.

Now, though, he was in serious trouble. Christmas was only three days away and he was personally responsible for ruining the holiday for his wife, something he really hadn't intended to do. His only chance was to find Elf before June got home. He slogged back to the house in his ruined suit, left his wrecked shoes outside the back door, stripped off his jacket and shirt as he went upstairs, and pulled on a pair of jeans and an old sweatshirt in the bedroom. Puppies have really short legs, Dan thought hopefully; how far could he get? Back downstairs, he slipped on a jacket and grabbed the flashlight he kept under the kitchen sink. He walked back down the hall to go out the front door and circle around the neighbor's house into their backyard, where he assumed Elf was cowering under a bush or something. Just as he opened the front door, though, June walked up the steps. The party was over.

Dan gulped, his eyes wide. He tried a preemptive strike. "Hi, dear. How was the party? Elf escaped," he blurted as fast as he could. Then he tried to slide past her into the night.

"What?" she said.

"I said, 'Elf escaped' and I'm going out to look for him." He ducked his head and squeezed past her through the doorway.

"My God," June scolded angrily as he went down the front steps. "How did you..."

Dan didn't wait to hear the rest of her question. "Get a flashlight and come on!" he called over his shoulder as he rushed away. He knew there would be further discussion later. This, his latest crime, would confirm June's conviction that he could not be trusted to follow even the simplest instructions without close, vocal supervision. But he was used to it. Don't get me wrong, Dan often said, June is not an unreasonable woman, she's just intense.

~ ~ ~

It was late, it was dark, it was cold, but roaming around outside wasn't so bad. December nights have the finest skies of the year so a heaven full of stars sparkled above Dan's head. There had been a little rain a few days ago, but no snow so far this year; the yards were damp but not sloppy. The crisp air cleared his head and his blood started to race with the thrill of the hunt. He went around to the neighbor's backyard, softly calling Elf's name and whistling in what he hoped was a friendly, harmless tone. But Elf didn't answer. He crouched to shine his light under the bushes and along the fence that divided the two yards. No Elf. He searched the other side of his neighbor's house, working his way back around to the front. Still no Elf. A light came on in the house above him. His neighbor, John Rantze, stuck his head out the window looking for a burglar he was sure he heard in his bushes. Dan waved vaguely at Rantze and hurried away.

Just as he got back to the front yard, someone in the street shone a spotlight in Dan's face. It was his other next-door neighbor, Jerry, with his wife Theresa, who was wielding a handheld spotlight. More flashlights came down the sidewalk from both directions. June had alerted the rest of the neighborhood and a posse had been formed. Dan figured she told them there would also be a lynching after they found the dog.

The neighbors gathered on Dan's porch and June soon had them organized. They spread out to search the area. They were a hearty bunch fueled by the excitement of the hunt not to mention the eggnog they had been enjoying all evening at the caroling party. Dan heard laughter and happy chatter between the calls of "Here, Elf" and "Here, puppy" echoing along the dark street. Occasionally there was a thump and an "ouch" followed by a drunken giggle from some searcher who had walked into a tree. A garbage can crashed somewhere across the street.

More lights came on along the block as other neighbors looked out to see what the disturbance was about. A few joined the hunt in their robes and slippers, as much to protect their shrubbery and flower beds from the stumbling search party as to find the missing dog. John Rantze kept them informed of the time by shouting it very rudely out his bedroom window.

Dan soon teamed up with Jerry, who had taken the thousand-candlepower spotlight from his wife and was having a great deal of fun turning its glare on the other people searching up and down the block. "You just blinded Dorothy Maguire," Dan warned him as the beam startled an elderly woman carrying a butterfly net. "Look for the dog, would you?"

"Which dog? The one you lost?" Jerry kidded as he swept the beam over John Rantze's windows and down into his shrubbery. Suddenly he stopped and held the light on a lurking figure in a hooded coat. "Hey, who's that?" he asked Dan. As Dan squinted through the dark, the person scurried out of sight around the corner of the house.

"I couldn't see the face," Dan said. "I caught a glimpse, but she didn't look familiar."

"I'm not so sure it was a woman," Jerry said.

"Well, if it wasn't that damn dog, I don't care," Dan answered. "Give me that thing, would you?" He took the light from Jerry's hand and swept it toward the street just as a police cruiser turned the corner. The car skidded to a halt as the driver was blinded by Dan's piercing light. The cop jumped out of the car shielding his eyes. It was one of Harrington's finest, Officer Miller.

"Kill that light!" he shouted. Dan fumbled with the switch until he got it turned off. "What's going on here?" Officer Miller demanded.

A crowd of searchers gathered around to explain—all at once. The cop listened to the babble for a minute, then said, "It's a little late for you folks to be out playing hide-n-go-seek. If you haven't found the dog by now, you're not going to find it tonight." The search party grumbled and milled around the police car. A couple of the less intrepid searchers drifted away.

"There's also a dark stranger prowling around," Jerry added. He hiccupped softly.

"Okay, so what did he look like?" Officer Miller said.

"We, uh, couldn't tell," Dan answered. "I think it was a man."

"It could have been a woman, though," Jerry added helpfully. "But they were definitely wearing a hooded coat,"

The cop looked around the small group, where three people had hoods pulled up against the December night. "Right. Come on, folks, let's all go home and sleep it off," he ordered. "You can look some more in the morning."

Jerry pointed to his watch and burped. "It's 12:17 AM, officer. That makes it officially morning right now."

"If you don't go home, sir, tomorrow you're going to need a proctologist to tell you what time it is," Officer Miller said through clenched teeth. That ended the search for Elf that night. It would resume the next day.

More About Hunting Elf

A puppy for Christmas? What could be better! Dan McCoy and his capable wife June find out when Santa gives them a frolicsome hairball named Elf, a Silky Terrier with champion bloodlines and the table manners of Groucho Marx at a Hunter S. Thompson New Year's Eve party. He's also on the wish list of nefarious dognappers who want to steal him as part of a murderous plot to win Westminster's "Best In Show." Elf foils everybody's plots, though, and brings Macy's Thanksgiving Day Parade to a tumultuous halt in the process. Hunting Elf is a comedic canine Christmas adventure.

"Donelson fills the novel with experiences recognizable by anyone who has ever raised a puppy. Elf lifts his leg in all the wrong places, chews on everything from an heirloom Oriental carpet to the CATV cable, and has an uncontrollable urge to dig up and eat delicacies like kitty paté, which gives a whole new meaning to the term 'doggie breath.'"

--The Larchmont Gazette

ISBN 978-1456315924

www.huntingelf.com

Available in print and ebook editions from your favorite book retailer. Audiobook edition read by the author available from Audible.com and iTunes.

Also by Dave Donelson…

Heart Of Diamonds:
A novel of scandal, love, and death in the Congo

Corruption at the highest levels of government, greed in the church, and brutality among warring factions make the Congo a very dangerous place for television journalist Valerie Grey. Amid the bloody violence of that country's endless civil war, Grey uncovers a deadly diamond-smuggling scheme that reaches from the heart of the Congo to the White House by way of an American televangelist. Heart Of Diamonds is a fast-paced tale of ambition, avarice, betrayal, and love.

"An absolutely brilliant must-read book. Dave Donelson captures the essence of the Congo's challenges. His Heart Of Diamonds is the modern corollary to Joseph Conrad's Heart of Darkness. Dave breaks the silence about the conflict in the Congo and firmly stands with the Congolese people in their quest for peace, justice, and human dignity."

--Kambale Musavuli, National Spokesperson, Friends of the Congo.

ISBN 978-1449919924

www.heartofdiamonds.com

Available in print and ebook editions from your favorite book retailer. Audiobook edition read by the author available from Audible.com and iTunes.

Blind Curve and other stories light and dark

Fifteen short stories in various genres.

Bad things happen in "The Alley," a tale told by a narrator who should know—he did some of them. Or did he? Only the victims can answer that question, and they're not talking.

Man's best friend offers the ultimate proof of his loyalty in "Bad Dog." The cute little canine doesn't care whether his master is a good man or an evil one, he simply obeys.

Benon Otema is not a criminal, he's just ambitious. A stalwart leader of his village, a successful merchant, a father and good provider, Benon should know better than to listen to tales told by a drunkard. But he does, and the story takes him to the "Blind Curve."

ISBN 978-1466396760

Available in print and ebook editions from your favorite book retailer.

Dave Donelson's
Dynamic Manager Guides & Handbooks
www.thedynamicmanager.com

**The Dynamic Manager's Guide To Marketing &
Advertising: How To Grow Sales And Boost Your Profits**
ISBN 978-1453889602

**The Dynamic Manager's Guide To Creative Selling:
How To Make More Sales And Build A Super Sales Career**
ISBN 978-1460929667

**The Dynamic Manager's Guide To Practical Management:
How To Manage Money, People, And Yourself To Increase
Your Company's Profits**
ISBN 978-1463782054

Dynamic Manager Handbooks

20 titles, short, to the point, and bargain priced in your favorite ebook format. Save time and money while focusing on the business skills that matter most to you.

Dave Donelson presents entertaining, informative programs for groups of all scopes and sizes. Custom editions of any of his books can also be created for your group. Visit www.davedonelson.com.

Made in the USA
Charleston, SC
25 May 2012